I0525048

THE WOLF

THE WOLF

Published by

For information, please contact:

JAG Publishing

Jagpublishing.org

Author's Contact Information:

Website|| Email

www.amandagrihm.com || amanda@amandagrihm.com

This is a work of fiction based on truth.

LCCN: 2003100326

Printed in the United States of America

THE WOLF

Amanda Grihm

Editors:
J. Emil Grihm
Janice Aaron-Whitley
Sara Hogue

JAG Publishing

Atlanta, GA

ACKNOWLEDGEMENTS

I could not have written this book without the love and support of my husband, J. Emil – affectionately known to me as Sweet, and my best friend, Janice. They have gone beyond the call of duty in helping me to delve back into the past and bring forth the details of the Wolf as I experienced him. Their encouragement and editing has been invaluable.

To my husband, Sweet, I can only say I know God has a reason for doing things the way He does and we are not in position to question the why's or why not's of His plan. I thank God for bringing you into my life at the exact moment he did. I praise Him for the strength of character He endowed you with and the loving husband that you are. I love you with all of my essence, my existence and my soul. Everything in my heart is there for you. I love everything about you, I have from the day I met you and I will until the day I die. You are a wonderful husband, a good friend, a strong protector and a great provider. You are down-to-earth, exciting, fun and intellectual. There is nothing I could have dreamed of that you do not bring to my table. You are everything man was meant to be and everything I ever wanted in a man!

To my best friend, Janice, I can't begin to tell you how much your friendship and love has meant to me. I love you like I love my blood-born sisters and brothers. I treasure your friendship and value your thoughts, ideas and advice. You have always trusted and believed in me and I have always trusted and believed in you. You never made me feel awkward or embarrassed when I had strange and weird experiences. You are a rare and beautiful person, a woman to be admired and cherished. You always helped me through the tough parts of my life and I will forever love you for being the sister, good person and great friend that you are.

I thank and praise God for the loving parents that raised me, Warren and Sara Nadall, both of whom are deceased but whose guidance, trust and faith shaped me into the person I have become. I could not have asked for a better life. I regret I didn't live up to the standard of trust you set in providing safely for me. I should have shared everything that was going on in my life with you. I should have known a child could not protect its parents; a child must allow the parents to be his or her protectors. Because I didn't do that, I missed out on a more beautiful relationship than what we had and I allowed a dangerous element to enter your lives as well as remain in my own.

Throughout my life and even though my mother remarried, I have always had the love, care and support of her first husband, Robert Johnson. I thank you so much for loving me like the rest of the kids and never showing a difference.

This book would not be complete if I didn't acknowledge the undying, unconditional love and support I have always received from my brothers and sisters: Bill (William Brown of Columbus, OH), Poochie (Raymond Brown of Toledo, OH), Oscar (Oscar Brown of Colorado Springs, CO), Toot (Terrence Brown of Cleveland, OH), Burma (Burma Burwell of Toledo, OH), Marcia (Marcia Crosby of Youngstown, OH), Marie

(Maria Elizabeth Crosby of Youngstown, OH), Libby (Sara Hogue of Toledo, OH), and their wives and husbands, my nieces, nephews, cousins, aunts and uncles. There are just too many to mention by name.

I have to acknowledge my brothers: Bill, who has been both the big brother and father to all of us. I wish I could do or say something that would give you back some of the childhood you missed when you took on the chore of caring for your siblings. I cannot help but cry for the childhood that was taken away from you. It was not fair for a child to take on the responsibility of helping to raise his siblings. I am forever grateful to you for your sacrifice to all of us. I love you dearly. Poochie, my cool brother with the swag that made us all run to the window just to watch every time you walked or ran down the street. You have always been a strong, loving force in my life. I think the first time I ever remember being proud was when Libby and Oscar took me to the window to watch you, "make it." Oscar, my star athlete and co-conspirator...You made our lives fun, crazy and exciting. All of my early adventures started with you and Libby. I have a good sense of humor and a great deal of pride because of you and I love you for that. Toot, my baby brother...and yes, my baby boy! We grew up closer than anyone because for so long it was just you and me. You advised me as much as I advised you. You are gone too soon and my heart breaks daily. I love you like I would a son, and as much as I still talk to you...I miss being able to call you. Yes I treated you like a baby. I was always so proud of you. Regardless of what troubles you faced, you remained a good strong man. A good brother, a good father for Hounchiepoonch and a good friend to me and everyone you came across. You had strong ethics that drove you and good will toward everyone you came across. I respect and will always admire those things in you. Remember, I rubbed Maumee's stomach when you were in it and asked to have you...she told me I could...and since that day, you were my baby.

To my sisters: Marcia, my beautiful songstress. I cherish the times that we all spent together. You were married most of my life and you passed on much too soon. I still hear your melodic, soft, soprano voice singing songs by Billie Holliday and Lena Horne...and I just love the sound, your sound! Burma, my sweet, strong sister that stands against the wind and protects every one of us with a soft, comfortable touch that will never let any harm come to any of us. You have always been so sweet and quiet. You laugh instantaneously just like Maumee. I don't think I've ever hear a foul word or bad thought about anyone come from you. I want to be more like you...quite, sweet and strong... I love you because you are such a good, loving sister... and such a strong loving part of our family. Marie, I can't even begin to talk about how much fun and craziness I experienced with you. You were so fass(yes fass...)and cool growing up. I wanted to walk and talk just like you. Now that you are put that behind you, you are a great example of a good Christian woman. You are still kind of crazy and I love you for all the great things I've had a chance to witness in you and learn from you. Libby, you are my best friend and my sister. You have stood up for me and fought for me and helped me my entire life. It was you, Toot and me...that talked daily...that strategized over hare-brained schemes and that came to our senses. You are so much a part of my life that I cannot imagine what my life would be without you. This book would not have been complete if you had not helped edit it. I love you dearly.

It has always brought me a great deal of pride and pleasure to acknowledge the good and thoughtful people that I have the honor to call my siblings. We are good, strong people with a compassion for others and that makes us rich in truth and spirit.

CHAPTER ONE

He started coming around about thirteen years ago. Our first encounter took place in a dream. I was lost, sitting on the ground in the middle of the woods. I marveled at the uninhibited wildlife and for the first time in my life I didn't envy the freedom others seemed to enjoy so much, and I longed to experience. I looked into the dense mass of trees and watched the animals play. I saw birds singing, lighting and flitting from one branch to another. There were nests with baby birds waiting to be fed by their mothers and spider webs that glistened from the touch of a ray of sunlight. The webs were larger than any I'd ever seen before yet they were intricately and delicately crafted. They were so magnificent you would have thought that only a master artist could have imagined and brought to life such beautiful designs.

With an overwhelming feeling of comfort and great satisfaction I nestled into the ground and lay bare on the long, wet blades of grass. The grass was so tall it almost covered my body. It was still wet from the morning dew yet its blades were sharp and cutting. Still, to the animals that occupied the plain it was comforting and restful.

In that moment, I became more aware of the artistry and beauty of an untouched nature. My surroundings were both provocative and soothing. Everything had a meaning and a specific purpose...even the dead carcasses that lay decaying on the ground. They would fertilize and feed the earth so the plants and trees would grow healthy and strong and all the animals of the world would have the vital foods they need to exist. I thought long and hard about life and how everything came to be. I realized the hands of God had beautifully crafted the scenery and everything in it...including me. Everything was pure, clean, and unharmed by the effects of man.

A feeling of dread and alarm raced through me for an instant. I sat upright; perfectly still, unsure of whether I was capable of moving or what I should have been doing at that moment. I looked at the lower part of my body but I wasn't sure of what I was seeing. I can only assume now what I saw were my legs. I was cold and an overwhelming weakness saturated my lower body. It was numb and didn't feel like it was a part of me. I looked up at the sky and, again, for a moment, I got caught up in the beauty and freedom of the life forms around me. The insects and birds flying through the air, large and small animals, and what seemed to be millions of micro biotic organisms moving through the grassy plain captivated me. The trees were alive and waving in the warm, soft breeze that blew over me. I felt the life-giving energy of the sun as it gently warmed and caressed me. The birds circled the sky and whistled soothing sounds that made me feel rested and comfortable.

The invasive steps of an intruder rudely interrupted the sounds of nature - the birds singing, the wind blowing and the numerous sounds made by the animals in the wooded area. And, even though the dew moistened the grass I heard crackling sounds, twigs snapping and leaves being crushed. The birds screamed out warnings of the intruder and flew away in flocks. There were so many birds they created a dark blanket across the sky as they moved away. Still I sat there. A strange feeling, a combination of calm, fear and strength came over me and I listened attentively for any sound that was not a natural part of my environment. Directed by my sense of smell I turned and looked to the south in the direction of the dense trees. I sat perfectly still and waited for the intruder to emerge and come to me.

I relaxed my body and lay flat with my face next to the ground and studied the shadows. All but one was familiar. It was as tall as the trees but it was not still like the trees. It moved … and it was moving toward me. The closer it got to me the smaller it grew in size. It was the shadow of a man, a tall, thin man who suddenly was standing in front of me. This man stood as rigid as a tree, looking down on me and grinning with every tooth in his mouth showing. His teeth were small, jagged at the edges and somewhat malformed. They were bright yellow and muted green with big splotches of brown on some of them. Many of them were chipped and ragged but they shined and glistened like they had been polished. The stranger stood in front of me for a long time before he said or did anything. After what seemed to be eternity he sat down next to me. Still, he didn't say a word. Tears streamed down my face without warning and uncontrollably. I was not afraid but I knew I was in danger. The man looked into my eyes and smiled even harder than before. He smiled so hard the edges of his mouth stretched taunt from one end of his face to the other.

He slowly and ceremoniously twisted and squeezed both of his hands together and held them in front of my face. He acted as though the movement of his fingers and hands was supposed to mean something to me. He twisted the fingers of his left hand around his right, squeezing all of his fingers down except the one he used to point at me. He squeezed his hand so tight that his knuckles and fingernails turned white. I stared at his finger as it moved close to my face. I watched it as though I had no choice and until my eyes crossed. He touched my face and followed the pattern of my tears. The man's smile slowly left his face. He, instead, had a look of intensity and determination in his eyes. I felt like he was looking inside of my soul. His eyes pierced mine. I tried to turn my head away from his enslaving gaze but I could not move. The man pressed his finger firmly under my eye. His hand was hot and soft but his touch was fiery, firm and forbidding. The heat from his hands reached me before his finger touched me. The wetness of my tears sizzled and dried and my skin burned from the intensity of the heat. He meticulously followed the pattern of my tears and erased them away, leaving a bruise and scar to mark the places where his finger touched me.

Before I knew it this man had cupped my chin in the palm of his hand and guided my face over and up so close to his I could not tell if it was my breath or his that warmed my nose. His eyes twinkled like stars. A smile crept oddly from one side of his face to the other until all I could see were glistening teeth and crinkled, twinkling, almost closed eyes. I wondered if he was a friendly force coming to my rescue or an evil force coming to destroy me. The firmness of his grip began to intensify. It became frightening and unyielding. I tried to resist and push him away but I felt as though I had no resistance in me. Still, he had my chin cupped in his hand and I could not open my mouth. My teeth were firmly clasped together. I tried to scream out, No...leave me alone, but his grip was much too strong. I tried to pull away from him and move my head from side to side to indicate my displeasure and uneasiness with this stranger but he had such a firm grip I couldn't move. He placed his other hand on the back of my head and in one swift movement he pulled me to an upright position, face-to-face with him.

This stranger with the brownish, leather-like skin pulled me closer, his grip became stronger and his strange smile turned into a twisted frown. He opened his mouth as he drew me nearer and he acted like he was trying to eat me, whole. Quickly, he took his hand from behind my head and grabbed my body. Oddly, my fears began to diminish and I felt like I had more control over him than he had over me. My lower body was no longer limp; it was strong. I could feel my strength surging, almost bursting, throughout every muscle. For the first time since our encounter I looked at this man knowing I had the upper hand. He glared fearlessly back into my eyes yet the twinkle in his eyes had gone away. His eyes were opened wide. They were as large as the acorns that fell from the trees. They were wide with a bodacious challenge in them. I moved closer to the man's face so I could look directly into his eyes and accept his challenge. Upon closer examination I could see that there was something in the center of his eyes. Whatever it was, it looked like small galaxies where several hundred stars orbited around some source of energy, a dark energy. Still, I readied myself to meet his challenge, whatever it was. I felt more in control than ever and I also began to feel more like a predator than a victim.

I watched with interest as this man raised his arms up in the air and cupped the top of his head this time. Quickly, he turned as though he was about to leave. Just as quickly as he turned I felt the hard ground meet and punish my body like I had been slammed and thrown onto it. Within a few seconds I was again looking at the man, eye-to-eye. In the next moment I was on the ground again but this time I had not been dropped or thrown, it was where my will led me to be.

I felt an odd, warm, fullness in my mouth and I saw blood shooting from the man's leg. Instinctively, I wrapped myself around him and began to squeeze him. I looked down at his feet and saw the tail of a large snake moving from side to side. I was not afraid. I was excited and empowered. The man's eyes were opened wide and the reflection of a gigantic black and yellow diamond-backed snake stared at me. I stared at the reflection in his eyes for a few minutes, admiring the sheer beauty and strength of that magnificent snake. I was fearless, my confidence and desire had become one...control. The man's mouth opened and I could see the outlining of hundreds of spirits being released into the air. To the human eye, it would have appeared he opened his mouth and nothing came out of it. But, being a part of the animal kingdom I saw what no man could see...the spirits that had been locked up inside of him had just been released upon the world.

Like a constrictor, I held him and he could not escape my grip. I squeezed him until he fell to the ground. I held him tight until the pounding of his heart and the pulsation of the blood moving through his veins had stopped. Even after he stopped moving I squeezed him. I kept on squeezing him until I heard bones snapping. I stopped this man from moving altogether almost the way he stopped me from moving earlier. I held him until the bones in his neck were crushed and the weight of the blood in his head pulled it down and caused it to swing aimlessly from side to side. His body became heavier as the blood drained from the top of his head and body down into his trunk, legs and arms. I continued to squeeze him even though his body had been limp and lifeless for hours. I heard a loud pop as my mouth stretched open and my jawbones unhinged. I put the man's head in my mouth and crushed it until all of the bones had collapsed. I felt his shoulder blades scrape the roof of my mouth so I squeezed him until his shoulder bones were also crushed flat and small. Each movement I made sucked more of the man's body into my mouth and further down my throat. Each movement caused the man to be crushed into smaller and smaller pieces. I devoured his entire body and when there was nothing left of the man I slithered away.

As I moved away, I felt stranger and stronger than before and I felt another transformation come upon me. I was moving through the grass quickly. I was not flying but it felt like I was running on air. Lifted by the strength of my confidence and moving by the will of my spirit, I was unfettered by the chains of conformance, fear, doubt, and anxiety. I was free to follow my instincts. I blinked for a second and when I opened my eyes I was looking at a large brown hairy snout in front of my face. It looked like the snout of a dog but instinctively I knew it was the snout of a wolf. I had a strange feeling, like I was on the inside, looking out, of this ferocious animal. My vision had become keen and perfect and I was seeing the world around me through round yellow orbs and experiencing life with a newfound confidence. I was strong and graceful and I ran so fast through the woods that everything I saw blended into beautiful streams of colors. I felt amazingly secure and undeniably in control. Everything was familiar. All of my senses - sight, smell, hearing, taste and touch - were enhanced a great deal. I was guided by my keen sense of smell. I smelled the aroma of things familiar and unfamiliar. I know now I smelled the aromas of creatures, foods, gases, and metals. I saw a blur of bright lights in the distance.

Within minutes, the blur crystallized into the image of a city. It was thrilling and exciting. I saw shiny cars, trucks, and buses speeding through the streets and creatures of every kind engaged in every imaginable activity. And, at last I was finding my way home. At that point, though, I didn't know what or where home was. Still, I was anxious to get there.

I ran faster and faster. My stride was long and steady. The force of my back legs pushed me harder and farther, closer and closer to the lights. The closer I got, the more powerful I became. My shoulder blades were enormous and they moved with precision like the gears of a finely crafted Swiss watch. As I slowed down I began to see the beauty of my powerful physique in the shadow that moved along side of me and in the reflection of the glass in the cars and windows I passed.

I saw creatures walking, sprinting and running. I ran toward the creatures but they ran away from me as though they were afraid. I didn't want to hurt them. I was curious. I merely wanted to see them. I wanted to see what kind of creatures they were. I wasn't hungry and I didn't sense I needed to defend myself so they had nothing to worry about. The only time I killed was when I needed food or needed to defend myself. Still, the closer I got the more they ran away from me. The ones that didn't see me kept coming toward me but when they saw me they stopped moving, altogether. Some of them looked as though they could not move. Others stopped abruptly but then they moved very deliberately and cautiously and turned to go in the opposite direction. They all looked very strange to me. They were obviously at the lower end of the food chain. They had no discernable strength. They looked weak, like field rodents - food. They stood on two legs and what would have been their front legs hung like limp branches from trees. They didn't have hair to cover their bodies and warm them during the cold months or cool them during the hot times of the year. Their teeth were small, blunt on the edges and didn't look as though they could sink into or tear meat. These creatures were inadequate and that was unappealing. Their mouths moved and strange sounds came out. Many of the ones walking and sprinting began to run. They communicated in a manner I didn't understand. They touched and grabbed each other, they wailed and whined and they ran away clutching desperately to each other. This made no sense because, ultimately, they slowed each other down and made it easier for me to get them, if that was what I had chosen to do. They, simply, were not worthy of the chase and certainly not the effort.

One of the creatures took something strange out of its covering. It was small and insignificant to the eye but it had bolts of lightning inside of it. He pointed the instrument at me and the lightening came in my direction and almost struck me.

These creatures are weak but they were given the instruments of death. I am strong, given a natural ability to live and survive and they were given the instruments to potentially cause my death. Is this the way things are balanced? This is not balance...lightning strikes against me. I must create my own balance and reduce this threat. Total and complete elimination...it was the only answer!

I sensed heat and confusion in the air. It was the smell of aggression emitted from the creature that had the instrument of death. Perhaps the instrument only had one bolt of lightning. It was imperative I take control and eliminate the threat he held over me. I stopped to size him up. First, I crotched down low to the ground and then slowly forward. I moved cautiously in his direction. I lowered my head, almost down to the ground, but I kept my eyes locked on him. I could feel and suddenly hear a deep-seated growl that moved through me. It began in my stomach and traveled through my body until it made my mouth curl and gripe as it passed over my tongue and exposed my long, sharp teeth.   The creature's mouth opened and his instrument dropped. The loud screeching sound he made and the loud clanging sound of his instrument hitting the ground created a noise that disturbed me. It made my teeth ring shrill.

The instinct to preserve my life was upon me. I began to move to the pounding of my heart. The beat was strong and it rang in my ears like herds of stampeding animals running from a burning forest. I had so much strength I felt like I was increasing in size. My paws stretched out wide and my claws suddenly shot forth. They were steady and strong like steel spikes. Within a few seconds I had planned my attack. There would be no escape for that creature. I moved into position to strike. Keeping him locked within my sight, I lifted my head as I stretched my strong shoulders low to the ground and then back toward my hind legs. My hind legs were unmovable. They would power my lunge and spring me high into the air. At the right moment I would extend my forelegs to complete the lunge. I would land on top of him, sink my teeth into his neck and snap it in half. As I began to move forward, I tilted my head slightly to the left and downward, still keeping the creature locked in my view. I felt the hair on my back and shoulders begin to move like static electricity was running through it. My long, sharp teeth were in view and dripping with saliva. I felt my blood warming. It started in my paws, then it moved up through my legs and thighs, across my back and stomach, and finally up through my chest. As the blood began to warm my neck, the hair on the back of my neck and body separated and stood straight up instead of lying down and warming me. I was wet around the tops of my shoulders and back. I took a mighty leap toward the creature. His mouth opened wider than before and stranger sounds came out of it.   His eyes rolled up to the top of his head and his body flopped, limp onto the ground.

I began to feel strange again.   I was caught up in the middle of my lunge. My strength was dissipating.   I took a long leap expecting to instantly land on the creature but instead of moving at a ferociously fast pace I was suddenly moving in slow motion, twirling around in a circle. The top of my head felt blocked and my nose and mouth were numb.   My eyes were blurry and burning.   I felt as light as a feather and I moved effortlessly as though I had been lifted by the wind.   As I moved closer to the sidewalk I felt the transformation complete.   I landed gently on the ground leading with the right foot as I had been taught in modeling school. As my heel touched the ground, my hand touched my face.   The snout and my strength were gone and my touch was as cold as ice.

In the next moment I woke in my bedroom.   The room was dark and the window was cracked open.   There was a mighty storm brewing outside that night. The winds were high and the cold wind from the north was blowing brown, dried leaves and debris into my room. My sheets, blankets and pillows were all wet. I was not sure of whether I had dreamed the whole thing or if I had experienced it. I knew one thing...if it was a dream it certainly didn't feel like one. It felt very real but I dismissed it by telling myself it was just a strange, ironic dream. It was ironic because I was always so frightened of animals and the possibility of the power people could exert over me. Yet, in my dream I became an animal and that was about the only time I could ever remember feeling comfortable with who and what I was. That was the only time I embraced my strength and the only time I knew that people had no power or control over me. I wanted that feeling again. I wondered if I had lived two lifetimes or if those creatures were living in me. I had often heard people talk about the nature of the beast in a person. I wondered if the wolf was the beast in me.

CHAPTER TWO

He came back about a year and a half later. This time I was not dreaming. It was the fall of the year and it had been unseasonably cold. The time had just moved back an hour so it got dark outside quicker. It was about seven thirty in the evening and the absence of light from the broken streetlights made it seem darker and later. It felt like midnight and it was almost pitch black outside. My car had been in the shop for repair for two weeks and I had to catch a bus to and from work each day. The bus let me off at the bottom of the hill on Euclid Avenue. To get home I had to walk about an eighth of a mile up Superior Hill. Superior Hill was a long, steep hill shrouded on both sides by woods where untamed animals lurked and dark towers with long, winding driveways hidden behind seven-foot high bushes and steel gates loomed.

Most nights I didn't mind the walk up the hill because another woman who lived in the building walked home with me each night. She and I talked so much about the lives of some of the people in the building it felt like we were at home a minute or two after stepping off of the bus. We were so caught up in the weekly gossip that fear never entered our minds. But, that day she didn't get on the bus...and I panicked. I was paranoid and frightened and I didn't want the bus to stop at all. I certainly didn't want to get off of it. I hated myself for being such a coward, for being so dependent upon everyone else for my safety. I hated the fact I was strangled by the possibilities of what could happen and I was held in a tight grip of fear because every little thing seemed to hold an ominous, treacherous ending for me in my mind. I dreaded the darkness of the night and the dark possibilities that lay ahead.

I saw another bus a few blocks away. I prayed the woman would be on that one and I waited at the bus stop with my fingers crossed and my eyes closed tight. I was deep in prayer when the bus pulled to the curve. I peeked through my eyelashes hoping to see her step off the bus. The driver stopped only to see if I wanted to get on. My heart felt like it had dropped to my feet. I shook my head, no, and I took a deep breath. As I lifted my head to measure the distance up the hill I could feel the fear take hold and begin to paralyze each part of my body.

After a few seconds, I felt totally and completely incapable of moving. I heard someone screaming, "You have to move. You can't stay here all night. Something will get you just as sure as your name is Sarissa. Come on girl, you don't have a choice. MOOOOOOOVE!"

The voice was so loud and clear it shook me and made me jump. I turned around in a complete circle looking for the person who screamed at me. No one was there...my mind was playing tricks on me...screaming at me, scaring me...but it gave me what I needed to move off of that spot.

My first steps were hard to make. My foot was heavy and my legs were wobbly and weak. It was difficult to move. I had a sinking feeling in the pit of my stomach and my head was light. My throat had a big lump in it and my hands were beginning to sweat. I tried to envision myself walking through the door of my apartment but my eyes kept scanning the dark street and dreary buildings that loomed over me. I took a big gulp and started to walk, fast, up the hill. As I moved farther up the hill and closer to my apartment I began to feel strange. Suddenly,

I was looking through bright, yellow orbs. I could see the large brown snout in front of my face again. The fear that had built up in me began diminishing until it disappeared altogether. A feeling of uninhibited power penetrated my being. I was bubbling over with confidence like a teapot filled to the brim, its water bubbling over when the water reaches the boiling point.   My mind was racing with new thoughts of courage and things to do on the way home. I wanted everyone to know how powerful and courageous I felt and I wanted to be seen and heard. I threw my head back and bayed loud to announce my presence to all who had ears to hear within a half-mile radius of where I stood. I felt my chest expand as I inhaled the cold air into my strong lungs. I could see my large, muscular, hairy shoulders moving in precision as I walked up the hill.   I felt free and strong. Without a doubt I was in control. My eyes were facing forward but I could see everything going on around me. I was happy to embrace the wolf this time. I slowed my gait so I could extend my time out and enjoy more of the cool, night air.   The darkness of the night was no longer intimidating nor was it frightening. The dark sky held more beauty, peace and security in it than ever before. The stars looked like bright white and blue diamonds strewn randomly across a black velvet backdrop and the moon was full and clear. I saw very few cars and hardly any people. I enjoyed every second of the time I spent walking up the hill that night.

I romped up the hill, frolicked on the sidewalk, ran into the woods and back out onto the street. I raced and chased the few cars I did see. I extended what would have been a five-minute walk into a twenty-minute adventure. My home was on the left-hand side of the street at the top of the hill. Out of fear and habit I always walked up the right-hand side of the road. I rationalized ... if someone were going to jump out of his or her car to try to grab me; they would have a hard time doing it. They were going to have to get out the car and run around to the other side to get their hands on me, unless they had someone sitting on the passenger's side that was strong enough to pull me inside. That was just one of the several fears that haunted me; and, one of the precautions I took when I walked alone. On this night, though, things were different and I was different. I courageously walked up the left side of the street.

I had to walk three blocks to get home. There was a neighborhood store and bar in the middle of the second block. I saw two men come out of the bar's door. Almost instantly my playful mood and my perception and understanding of the things around me had changed. All of a sudden I didn't have a destination. I was a free spirit moving through life. I understood home to be wherever I made it. And my view of the two men changed from men to creatures. They were strange and weak like the ones I had encountered more than a year ago and they were making the same kinds of strange sounds. Instead of running away from me these creatures were walking fast and running toward me. I remembered the one that had the instrument didn't run from me. It came toward me just as they were doing. I remembered the thrashing sound of the lightning that came from the instrument of death the creature pointed at me. I slowed my gait to see if either of them would pull one of those instruments of death from its coverings.

The negative, intense heat that emanated from the bodies of the two creatures disturbed the cold, brisk, air and reached me in seconds. Still, I could not understand the sounds they made. As I moved up the hill I became stronger. At first I lifted my head, slowly, and then I tilted it up and to the right. As I lowered my head their image crystallized. They moved in unison. The heat from their bodies intensified as they moved closer and closer to me. They increased the speed of their steps and I slowed mine. I knew they were going to break their pace and split up in an attempt to overpower me. One would get in front of me and the other would get behind me. The one that would get in front of me would be the stronger of the two, capable of engaging in a frontal attack. The one behind me would be weak and more likely to run once I killed the first one. Just as I had anticipated and no sooner than the thought had completed in my mind, they broke their stride and began to move at different paces. One ran a few steps ahead of the other and the other dropped back a few steps. This put them right in the position I had anticipated.

I planned to attack the one that would have been behind me first as he would have a better chance of escape - running downhill. Then I would run uphill and get the one who would have been in front of me. The first one stood approximately fifteen steps away from me and the second was a little more than twenty steps away. They were making very loud noises and waving at me. The heat from their bodies burned me like fire. This was an indication of an animal ready to attack. I went immediately into attack mode. I slowed my steps so I could more readily meet their challenge. I locked them within my sight. I could see my snout snarl, the saliva drip from the edges of my long, sharp teeth and I could feel the heat intensify and surge throughout my body. I felt my head lower as my shoulders moved forward. Still, I kept the creatures locked within my sight. I could feel and hear the bones crack in my shoulders as my powerful forelegs stretched low to the ground and forward to stabilize my position while pushing up and back on my back and stomach. My hind legs felt as powerful as galvanized steel and would again power my lunge. Suddenly, the one closest to me stopped moving. It began reaching backwards in an attempt to make contact with the other. The second creature stopped moving within seconds of the first. Instantaneously, the heat from their bodies began reversing.

Instead of emitting the fiery waves of negative energy directed toward me, the negative energy neutralized and the heat was turned in the opposite direction. This was an indication of fear. The first creature kept reaching back toward the second. His limbs flailed aimlessly backwards in an attempt to make contact. He made loud, familiar sounds, like those of prey that had accepted defeat because it knew there was no escape. I turned quickly and locked in on the eyes of the first creature. The second creature's lower legs were shaking, they moved apart and together at a very fast pace. By this time they were communicating with each other by screeching out high-pitched, loud sounds. The first one screeched louder and more often than the second. Because of the loud noises he made, I decided to get rid of that one first. That way, I would stop the disturbing sounds that made my ears ring shrill. They both turned and ran away from me. They looked back at me as they ran. Each time one of them looked back he would run into the other causing both of them to fall. Realizing I was no longer in danger of attack I continued to walk up the hill. I wanted to frolic in the cool of the night air. I held my head back as far as I could and bayed a loud salute to the moon, letting all know I had arrived. I was happy and I was in control.

The Superior Tower Apartments was upon me before I knew it. It was a huge building with thirty floors. I lived on the twenty-sixth floor and although it was in the City of East Cleveland I could see all the way to downtown Cleveland from my balcony. The building was one of the more modern apartment buildings in the city and the biggest bunch of wannabes in the entire state of Ohio occupied it. Most of the tenants were young and in very good shape. They worked out religiously and fanatically. The single tenants seemed to have fixations on two-seater sports cars, Afghan dogs, poodles and fox terriers. There was only one woman in the building with a cat. She was hated by all of the dog owners because she seemed to be able to dictate the times and activities the others could undertake just so she could walk her cat. The woman's name was Mary. She appeared to be a nice person, extremely intelligent and a great conversationalist. However, when it came to her cat she became irrational, stubborn, shortsighted and rude. She made such a fuss about the times the other tenants walked their dogs that management created a whole new set of rules on pet ownership for the tenants.   One person was evicted because he blatantly disregarded the new rules. I didn't have any pets because I was afraid of both dogs and cats.

As I stepped into the driveway I felt my strength dissipate and another transformation come upon me. I greeted two of my neighbors as they walked toward their cars. One of them, Pam, a very good friend stopped to talk. She wanted to know where the other woman was and offered to pick me up at the bottom of the hill in the future. She was worried because a few minutes earlier she and her husband heard what they thought was the howling of a big dog or maybe even a wolf. Pam had just had a new baby and, as small as he was, he was running her like a coach doling out laps to a football player for insubordination. Ricky was one of the prettiest babies on the face of the earth. He had jet-black hair and eyebrows, copper colored skin and the most perfectly shaped eyes, nose and mouth I had ever seen on a baby. Looking at him was like looking at a drawing or picture of what you'd image to be the most beautiful baby in the world. And, to look at him you'd think his tiny little mouth could barely open to let a sound out. My apartment was above Pam's and every time little Ricky cried I felt like running down to their apartment to see who was trying to kill him. That child's voice rang out like a bell from a cathedral bell tower on Sunday morning. Every time I saw Pam, she looked tired and sleepy. She wasn't accustomed to staying awake all hours of the night. She was the only person I knew who insisted on getting her beauty rest and was in bed by ten weekdays and midnight on the weekends.

Pam was tired, I could tell, but she insisted I allow her to pick me up at the bottom of the hill until I got my car back. I thanked her but adamantly refused her offer. My car was going to be delivered to me at the job in the next day or two so there was no need to inconvenience her. She had enough on her hands with little Ricky dictating her life. He ran her like a greyhound chasing one of those toy rabbits at the tracks. I told her I did see a big dog but he was friendly. That seemed to put her at ease. I also told her the dog had walked with me all the way to the driveway. Before I could say anything else or make up a story about him running back down the hill, she had jumped into her car and rolled up the windows. Pam was extremely afraid of dogs. I assured her this one would not have hurt her. I said it with so much confidence it made her take a second look at me. I tried to clean up my statement by saying he was extremely friendly and playful. I had to laugh at the thought of Pam, huddled up in her car with the windows rolled up; looking from one side to the other, knowing the animal she was afraid of was me. Any other time I would have been huddled up in that car with her.

CHAPTER THREE

My happy mood faded when I opened the door to my apartment building. Experiencing the wolf made me realize I had no freedoms at home. I felt trapped like a caged animal. It was a miserable, constrained existence and I wanted to feel free like the wolf. I got on the elevator but didn't push the button so I could savor the feeling of freedom a few minutes longer. Finally, I pushed the button for the twenty-first floor. I got off of the elevator and walked up the stairwell to the twenty-sixth floor just to extend the time before I'd have to go into my apartment. I exited the stairwell, turned to the right, took five steps and stood in front of my apartment door. I stood there and let out a long, belabored sigh as I stuck the key into the keyhole. I could hear the locks on my neighbor's door unlatch and the door creaking open. I looked over at his door and it was just slightly ajar. Still, I could see him peeking at me through the small crack in the door. The subtle scent of Aramis seduced my nostrils and filled me with pleasant thoughts of being held gently by the man of my dreams ... the one who had yet to exist in my life. I stuck my tongue out at him and he jumped away from the door, letting it open completely. I heard him fall over his furniture and curse as he hit the floor. Next I heard glass breaking and more cursing. I laughed at my neighbor as I turned the key. I let the door creak open slowly. The thought of going in saddened and frustrated me. I didn't want to face the dreary, unhappy life that awaited me. I wanted to go back outside and become the wolf again. I needed that feeling of freedom.

Through the small opening in the door I smelled the scent of an unclean woman drowning in Coco Chanel perfume. I swung the door open and there she was - an unclean woman sitting on my sofa. I wanted to scream, "You're supposed to wash your stinking butt before you put Chanel on." but I forced myself to smile at her. Next to her was Robert, my husband, Jerry's, best friend. Beads of sweat popped out of his forehead and he had a strange look on his face. The stinking woman sat there rolling her eyes up and down, looking me over. For a second my imagination took over and I saw myself slapping her so hard her eyes stuck in that position, at the top of her head looking up. I let out another long sigh but this time it was like a sigh of relief.   I didn't feel trapped like before nor did I feel the need to patronize them. Any other time I would have forced myself to be polite.   I would have offered to refresh their drinks and then I would have gone into another room to prepare the paperwork for the audition I was holding that night. This time it was different. I felt offended, fed up and I was not going to take it. I was not stupid and I wanted Jerry to know I knew what was going on.

Films of smoke covered the apartment and me. That stinking woman sat there puffing her stinking cigarette and looking at me as though I had no right to be there. The stink that covered her didn't mix well with the Chanel. I wanted to throw up when I walked into the room.   Music was playing low and the lights were dimmed. The stinking woman looked at me and smiled a devious, half twisted smile. Then she shook her head to rearrange her hair. She took her lipstick out of her purse, licked her lips and stared at me as she pretended to reapply her lipstick. She smacked and popped her lips, looked at me and started laughing. She put her lipstick back in her purse and settled back into my sofa in a way that made it look like she was becoming more comfortable and preparing for a long stay.   Still fixing his clothes, Jerry came, almost running, from the bedroom to greet me. He had a strange look on his face. The woman had a look of disdain on hers.

Jerry looked at the two of them and nervously said, "So, are we ready to go?" Then he looked at me and spoke as he exhaled a long sigh of relief, "I'll be home a little late. You got rehearsal tonight, don't you? I may come down there."

Jerry and Robert grabbed their coats and hurriedly put them on. They were rushing around like rats running from a cat but the woman took her time putting her coat on. She rolled her eyes at me, laughed a few times and moved slowly toward the door.

She was about to step into the hallway when I said, "Excuse me! Who are you?

She took a long puff from her cigarette, blew the smoke in my direction and exhaled as she spoke. "You don't want to know who I am."   She looked me from head to toe as she spoke and then she turned her back toward me and started walking toward the door again.

"I wasn't finished. And turning your back on me is not a good option for you right now, so look at me when I talk to you."

She stopped and dropped her cigarette on the floor, rubbed it into my carpet and turned slowly toward me. "Like I said," she whispered with a smirk on her face but in a low, angry voice. "You don't want to know who I am!"

By that time I had walked over and stood about an inch away from her. I thought about slapping her but decided against it. Instead, I said, "It is perfectly clear to me what you are! Now, I want to know who you are...as in what's your name and why are you in my apartment?"

She threw her hand up and motioned for me to step away from her. I stepped closer to her, so much so it was uncomfortable not just for her, but for me. I stood so close to her it forced her to take a step back. Robert laughed nervously as he put his arms between us and tried to wedge us apart. He couldn't get us apart so he jerked her arm and pulled her away from me. He finally got her far enough away to stand between us.

"She's with me, her name is Blascey."

I looked into her eyes almost daring her to move them away from mine. "Can you talk or are you dumb, Blascey?"

She looked at me with more hatred and arrogance in her eyes than I'd ever seen before.

"I ain't the dumb one," she snapped.

She tried to reach around Robert to hit me. She smiled a crooked smile and blew what remained of her stinking smoke in my direction again.

I shook my head to shake some of the stink off but her breath still seeped into my nostrils. Then I pinched my nose to stop the pervading smell from infiltrating my nostrils.

"Let me tell you just how dumb you are. You are sitting in my apartment with the smell of my husband all over you.   You didn't have the good sense or good grooming habits to wash yo' stinking butt before putting on Chanel.   I could hurt you really bad and no one would blame me for it.   Robert can't help you and Jerry won't help you if I decide to tear you apart, so I'd say you are dumb, pretty damn dumb."   I took my hand from my nose and turned my head toward the bedroom and sniffed. Next I turned toward the bathroom and sniffed and then I turned to face her again.   "I'd say you two were in the bedroom no more than five minutes ago and in the bathroom no more than three minutes ago.   So, if you think I don't know what you were doing here then, yeah, I'd say you are the dumb one here tonight."

She was filled with fear at first and then rage. Robert grinned a sheepish grin and pushed her farther away from me.

"The perfume was the mistake.   Smells like someone sprayed Chanel on wet dogs and garbage."   I fanned the air away as I spoke.

Jerry looked at me as though I had embarrassed him.   I was feeling good about this confrontation.   I had never confronted him or his indiscretions before nor had I ever aggressively confronted anyone. I was always defending myself or my position but this time being the aggressor felt good. I smiled at the thought of my newly found assertive behavior.

I turned to Jerry.

"Are you embarrassed because of something I've done? Are you seeing what's going on here tonight? If not, I certainly do!"

He shook his head in disgust. I had the urge to slap him and I did. I slapped him before I knew it and a battery of accusations and assertions came out of my mouth before I even realized it. I hit him with one question after another and one accusation after the other. Jerry was more embarrassed than ever and I sensed he wanted to slap me back. Instead, he stood there holding his face with one hand and fighting with himself to hold his temper. Blascey and Robert stood in the hallway looking at each other like they had just witnessed something that had never been done before.

Blascey shouted, "I don't believe this..." and Robert put his hand over her mouth before she could finish the sentence.

I ended my barrage of accusations with, "What you should be embarrassed about is the smell in this apartment. It smells like funky, wet, alley dogs and whores." I looked at Blascey and took a step toward her, she jumped back ... even to her own surprise. "A whore house," I said with deep disdain, "but you dogs like that smell don't you, Jerry?" I stared at Blascey while I spoke.

She jumped toward me again and Robert grabbed her. He held her back as if letting her go would result in her running over and beating me senseless. I told him to let her go. He slowly raised both arms as though I had just pulled a gun on him. She looked a little surprised. She was still angry but she never took another step toward me. Instead, she stood there with an angry look on her face and a hateful look in her eyes, puffing her stinking cigarette and blowing her stinking breath and smoke in my direction.

"I thought so, even if you didn't have the good sense to stay out of my house, you know better than to take another step closer. There is one thing, Blascey; I do want to thank you because you just bought my chains."

She growled out the words, "Don't say anything to me."

Before she realized she had left her purse on the table, I snatched it and threw it at her. It whizzed past her head and hit the elevator door. Everything in it was scattered on the floor. She had a look of disbelief and fear in her eyes. I zeroed in on the fear immediately.

I clenched my teeth and spewed out my words, "Get that crap off of the floor and away from my apartment before I rub your face in it."

She tried to say something but Robert put his hand over her mouth and held her next to the elevator. I heard the creaking of my neighbor's door as it moved open wide enough for him to peek out. Blascey stood still while Robert picked up her stuff. Every time she tried to move he shoved her back against the wall.

I turned slowly and looked Jerry up and down. I could feel his growing discomfort.

"Thank you, Jerry, you just freed me from this banishment to hell we called our marriage."

He had a sad look on his face. His words were filled with pain. "You don't mean that. You love me. You don't want this marriage to end."

I laughed and screamed at the top of my lungs, "You just bought your way out of this marriage and you just let me out of hell! Why on earth would I want a sentence to hell to go on forever? Why would I want to stay in hell when I could get out?" I turned to walk away but I had an afterthought. I turned back to him and laughed out the words, "I just can't thank you enough."

Jerry swung his arm back and raised his hand like he was going to slap me. I stood there defiantly looking at him and waiting for his hand to come close to my face. In those few seconds I had envisioned myself snapping his hand off and slapping him with it. He lowered his arm and stood there looking at me. I was standing directly in front of him, face-to-chest; I couldn't look at him face-to-face because he was so tall. I grabbed his arm and pushed him into the hallway without giving it a second thought.

I wasn't anxious or nervous but I was shaking when I said, "I don't want you in my life anymore. I want you gone, Jerry. I want you to leave here for good. I'm afraid if you don't leave, I'm likely to hurt you and it will be really bad."

I tried to shut the door but he stuck his foot in it and pushed it open. He was angry and wanted to hurt me mainly because of my words but I think a part of it was the fact he had big bunions on his feet and I had just slammed the door on one of them. I could see hatred in his eyes and I could feel his rage building.

He gritted his teeth when he spoke. "That sounds like a threat."

"No, it's not a threat." I whispered, "It's a promise!"

He took off his coat and walked back into the apartment. He flopped down onto the sofa. "I ain't going nowhere." Although angry, he had a sad look in his eyes, almost like he was remorseful for what had just happened.

Blascey and Robert were standing in front of the elevator. Blascey had one hand on her hip and the other shoved a cigarette in her mouth every few seconds. She was already angry but I could tell she was becoming angrier.

I looked at her and smiled, "Blascey, call your dog."

Robert said something to her that made her eyes buckle but she didn't say a word.

I repeated, "Blascey, call your dog. He doesn't want to go with you now. He may need a bit of prodding so call him, would you please?" I looked at Jerry and continued, "But, you can count on this, he's getting out of here and taking the hell he brought with him."

"Why don't you get to the point? Do you want to know if I was here with him?"

"You are dumber than I thought.   Did you hear any of what I said to you? Do you think I don't know you were?"

She grinned at me with one of those cats that ate the cannery looks.

"You and the smell in this apartment told me everything I could have ever wanted to know when I first walked in here." I said with a tone of relief and a bit of laughter.

It occurred to me then she actually thought I didn't know what was going on. I would have had to be mentally retarded not to see what was going on between them.

"Yeah, I ain't told you nothing, but I'll tell you this..."

Robert covered her mouth and pulled her backwards into the elevator.

I shook my head with disgust.   She bit Robert's hand and screamed, "Don't you ever put your damn hand on my mouth again.   Who do you think you are?" Then she looked at Jerry and growled out the words, "Are you coming or not? I am not up for this mess. I got things to do and I need to know what you gonna do."

Jerry had a look of disbelief on his face.

"See, it'll be an ice storm in hell before you three stooges outsmart me. Jerry, your whore is calling you. Go ahead; get out of here, you punk!" I said in the most arrogant tone I've ever used in my life.

Jerry touched my arm with one hand and covered his mouth with the other hand. He whispered, "She don't mean nothing to me. She's with Robert."

"Oh, she doesn't mean anything to you, Jerry? Why are you whispering?" I slapped him for touching me. "You must really think people become stupid when you want them to be. Not me, Jerry...not me."

Jerry grabbed both of my arms and squeezed them together.

"Don't you hit me again or I will hurt you. I will, I will hurt you and it'll be so bad you may not recover, you hear what I'm saying!"

Staring unflinchingly in his eyes, I responded with an unemotional, hard retort. "Get out of my face...and do it now. You are not a threat to me. Don't think you can do harm to me because you won't be able to stand up to the pain that will come along with that mistake!"

I was expecting to see the snout at any minute but it didn't come out. Blascey broke Robert's grip and started walking toward me. Still the snout didn't come out. Before I realized it, I had my hand around her throat and was choking her. I pushed her back over to the elevator. She tried, desperately, to open her mouth to say something.

"Say it... say anything... if you even blink, you will die in the dark! Blascey, you don't want to see how far I will go with this. Don't think for one minute I will not hurt you."

I pressed the button for the elevator and when the door opened I pushed her inside. Robert stood there, almost like he was in shock.

I turned to Robert and Jerry.

"You have until that elevator door closes to get out of my sight."

I heard a loud noise...Jerry had jumped out of the chair, put his coat on and ran into the elevator. As the door was closing he put his hand between the door and the infrared beam to stop it.

"I didn't do anything. She's with Robert." His voice was shaky and he had tears in his eyes as he spoke.

I jumped toward the elevator door and he jumped back and bumped his head against the wall of the elevator.

He pushed the button to open the door again.

"I'm telling you. I didn't do anything. I just wanted to go out with them."

"Well, what are you complaining about? That's what you're doing ... you're going out with them. But if I were you, I'd stop by the drug store and buy some soap."

Robert poked his head out of the elevator. He had a nervous giggle in his voice.

"You ain't upset with me are you?"

I ignored Robert and walked back into the apartment feeling both happy and sad. It was Wednesday and every Wednesday I held rehearsals for my modeling troupe, Panache Models. I had an hour before the rehearsal would begin. The phone rang. When I answered it there was only heavy breathing on the other end.

"Hello, hello, hello...I'm not in the mood to play games with anyone so speak up!"

The phone went blank and I heard dial tone. The phone rang again. I took it off the hook and laid it on the table. About five minutes later I heard a very light tap on the door. It was the man next door. We had been neighbors for two years and I didn't even know his name. I barely opened the door wide enough to see him. The scent of Aramis greeted me first and I lowered my defenses. I noticed how debonair he looked in his black and brown satin brocade smoking jacket and pants. The white brocade scarf was a bit much, though.   He had a bottle of Bollinger's Grande Année in one hand and a platter of grapes, orange slices, Kapiti cheese and crackers in the other. I opened the door wider and he walked past me and sat down on the sofa.   He put the Année and platter on the coffee table.   Then he stood up and stretched out his arms as though I was supposed to run into them and let him hug me until everything was all right. I took a deep breath, walked over to him, grabbed his arm, walked him back out the door and closed it.   I turned and saw his stuff on the coffee table so I gather everything, went to the door, opened it and threw all of it at him.

"Here, you forgot this."

I closed the door and sat on the sofa. This was sooooo unlike me.... But I loved it!

CHAPTER FOUR

I put the phone back in the cradle and it rang again, immediately. It was my Assistant Manager, James, telling me to bring the film so we could record the audition. It was close to eight o'clock and I still had to pull together some paperwork and get downstairs to the rehearsal hall. When I walked in the door six of the models were waiting for me. They had opened the hall, cleared away the chairs, made hot chocolate and put together routines they wanted the applicants to perform.

I was always happy when I got to spend time with the models. We had a lot of fun together and they were like family to me. They had two tables ready; one had a sign on it that read "Sign In Here" the other had a sign that read "Callbacks." Thirty-five people were auditioning that day so we had to be extremely organized. The screening process was very simple, normally. It would consist of the applicants introducing themselves so we could get an idea of what their speaking voice was like. They would perform straight runway with a few turns so that we could gage their poise and posture and then they would be asked to model as one of our seasoned models described their outfits so we could see how well they showed clothes and followed along with the commentator. This time, however, the applicants would do a few turns, mannequin modeling, coordinate switches, tearoom and runway. When I saw that list I knew the models really didn't want anyone else to join the troupe. I glanced over at Sophie and shook my head. She smiled but turned her head quickly so I would not see her laugh. If I had had those same requirements for them only one or two would have made it. I stared at her until she looked back at me. We both laughed.

"You know you're too much."

"They need to be sharp coming through the door. We have a show a month and we don't have time to train anybody."

"Maybe we need to have a day for training and get a trainer. We all know more than half of you didn't know how to do a mannequin or tearoom."

Her large eyes, with the half-inch lashes, opened and closed slowly as she spoke, "They better be sharp, that's all I have to say. You know they are out there representing me when they wear the name Panache."

Sophie was my best model. She was a good friend and she worked hard to make sure our routines were exciting and professional. I understood exactly where she was coming from. She stopped talking abruptly, looked me squarely in my eyes, ran over to me and hugged me.

She whispered in my ear, "Something is not right, do you need me to do anything? I know you and something is going on!"

I smiled at the thought she was so in tuned with me. I didn't think anybody but my best friend, Aleena, could read me so well. I couldn't hide anything from Aleena and she couldn't hide anything from me; and, it wasn't like we ever tried to hide anything from each other.   We may have held back on small bits of information for a couple of hours but by the end of the day we would have spilled our guts to each other two or three times over.

Aleena could tell by the tone of my voice when something was going on and vice versa. We knew each other like a book we had read 'til the pages fell out. We could anticipate each other's reactions as though we had already known what was going on. It was good to have at least one person I could be totally honest with and that same person who I never had to explain anything to. I didn't think anyone but Aleena could just look at me and know what I was thinking or feeling, but Sophie obviously knew me better than I thought. Her eyes were big and they were roaming my face looking for more signs of distress.

Finally, I shook my head, no. "You're right, something is going on, but there's nothing you can do."

Big tears welled up in her eyes and sat conspicuously on the top of her bottom eyelids, clinging on and almost spilling over for several seconds. She tried to hold back the tears but when the first one fell it seemed like the floodgates opened and a dam of tears burst out and streamed down her face. Sophie was a very strong-willed person but she was also extremely sensitive and would cry at the thought of a cartoon cat being stuck in a tree. She grabbed me and squeezed me so hard I felt my heartbeat in the top of my head. Because we were all so close and Jerry was a part of Panache I felt it would be best to let everyone know what was going on. I made the announcement I was contemplating a divorce.

Before I could finish, they were all jumping up and down for joy.

James said, "I'm so happy to hear that ... now, maybe we can get somewhere. I don't know how many people have asked me when you were going to get rid of that albatross."

I was surprised at their reaction and it showed all over my face as I looked at each of them. I didn't know any of them felt that way, or that the problems I had been having with Jerry throughout our marriage were so obvious to everyone else.

Sophie started singing..."Ding, dong the witch is dead, the wicked witch, the witch is dead, ding dong the wicked witch is dead." She stopped abruptly, and said, "I'm sorry but I'm soooooooooooo happy to hear that. This is the best news I've heard in a long time. She continued singing, "Ding, dong the witch is dead. The wicked witch, the witch is dead." She stopped abruptly again, this time she pointed to the door and said, "Look, the damned thang done resurrected."

Sophie walked over to James, tapped him on the shoulder and motioned for him to move. She sat down next to me and leaned over and whispered, "Don't pay him any attention. Oh, and I can't be intimidated into moving like James."

Jerry walked up to us and stood over Sophie as though he expected her to jump up and let him have her seat. She looked up at him and rolled her eyes. She made a sweeping, brushing movement with her hand, telling him to move out of the way. Jerry went to the next table and pulled out a chair and straddled it. He sat there staring at Sophie like he expected his glare to make her move. Sophie let out a loud snuffing sound and moved around as if she was settling more comfortably into her chair.

I smiled and thanked her. She was my own little mother hen. I hadn't really noticed it before, but she was very protective of me. I was always uncomfortable when Jerry hung around during our rehearsals. Sophie tapped into my discomfort and always seemed to be able to run interference. Josephine was another very good model and friend. I guess on that day my face must have shown some kind of hurt or pain, or more pain than usual, because it seemed as though every one of the models was trying to protect me from Jerry. Sophie and Josephine had some type of telepathy thing going. Sophie looked in Josephine's direction and she immediately took charge where Sophie normally would have. Josephine got Lena and three other models to hand out and check the applications, sign the models in and got the model releases while she and Stuart called out the routines. James and Danny worked the Callback table while Stephen filmed the auditions for review. It was a very smooth process.

The first model to come through the door was Dorothy. She weighed about three hundred pounds. She had a beautiful smile and enough confidence to fill the room. She had been a model for some of the Lady Michele ads. She was experienced in runway, print and television.

Jerry stood up and opened his mouth to say something but before the first word came out I interrupted him.

"Jerry, there are no band auditions tonight. You don't have to stick around for this."

He was angry. "I know this ain't no damn band auditions. I came to make sure we get the right kind of models in this troupe. And, I can see it is a good thing I did come."

I felt embarrassed for Dorothy. I knew she understood what he was insinuating. I told Sophie to take over. I walked over to Jerry and took his hand. I squeezed his hand so hard I could have sworn I heard his bones crack.

Before I could get him out the door he said, "You'll let anything in this group. We are the only troupe in town that let fat people model for us. I don't know what the hell I have to do to make you get some good models in this troupe."

I bent his finger back and walked him into the hall. There were so many people in the hallway I opened the first door we came to and went inside. It was the Men's Room. With strength that came from the heavens above, as soon as his foot stepped onto the Men's Room floor, I pushed him against the wall and held him there.

I was so angry I was shaking.

"A model is a representative of a group of people, Jerry. And you know what? People come in all sizes. Why do I find myself explaining this over and over to you?"

He looked like he wanted to hit me so I grabbed his wrist and bent his hand down so he couldn't move it. His eyes were filling up with more and more hatred for me. For some reason that surprised me and after about thirty seconds I let his hand go. He swung his arm back as if he was going to slap me. I hoped he would so that the wolf would come out and tear him apart. In a flash, I had envisioned blood splattering and pieces of him flying all over the room.

I stood in total silence trying to summons the wolf. For some reason he would not come out.

Jerry walked around in a circle as he spoke, "I know you want to represent everybody, but some people shouldn't be up there trying to model."

I wanted to throw up. I was beginning to dislike him so much he began to look ugly to me. I wanted to hurt him the way he hurt me and anyone else who didn't meet his off-base standards. I wanted to slap him until his face shook like Jell-O and fell off of his body.

I spoke very softly, "The person who should not be represented is the one who represents no one. One who is only concerned about his own interests, and one who cheats! A lying, stinking, self-serving cheat should not represent Panache Models. That's you, Jerry. You lying, stinking, self-serving cheat! You have no place here.

This is not something that you have a say in. This is my thing! This is not ours! You are not the owner! You were an afterthought!"

He tried to work up some tears but they just wouldn't come.

"I didn't do anything with her, she's Robert's woman. She just got a crush on me."

"Did you forget I was in the room? Did you see any of what happened in there? What? What? Do you think I'm that big of a fool?"

"Okay, I told you, she got a crush on me."

I slapped him for thinking I was so stupid and then I turned to walk away.

He grabbed my arm. "You can't keep slapping me 'cause you feel like it. I will hurt you!"

I slapped him again.

He said it again. "I will hurt you! I know that you are upset but you had better get over it. I'm going to be around whether you like it or not. I have never hit you but I have broken women's ribs in the past. So, don't think you can talk to me any kinda way and keep on slapping me."

He looked at me with a snarl in his nose and two of his teeth showing through pinched, rolled lips. He closed his eyes and hit the wall. It cracked. He opened his eyes slowly and unclenched his fist. Then he looked at me with even more hatred in his eyes. I just really wanted to make him feel the way he made me feel. I didn't hate him but I disliked him enough to want the wolf to tear him to pieces. Or, maybe I did hate him. One thing was for sure, I saw hatred in his eyes and that's when I realized he hated me! I could not understand why he wanted so badly to stay with me. He could start his own troupe if it was important to him.

He gritted his teeth when he spoke. "You better watch out, 'cuz you don't know what I might do to you." He turned to walk away and then he turned back and looked in my eyes without flinching and said, "And, you don't want to know how far I'll go with this! Right now I feel like I could kill you without giving it a second thought."

His hatred was oozing out of every pore in his body by this time. Strangely enough I was not afraid of this six foot seven inch giant. I welcomed the challenge!

I looked up at him and stared with as much hatred in my eyes. "Yeah, I guess we both better sleep with one eye opened because I'm in the same place you are. Hurting or getting rid of you wouldn't cause me one second of grief."

I could feel a growl emanate from deep in my spirit, it was about to come out when he grabbed me and tried to hug me. The hatred was gone from his eyes but this time he wanted sympathy and forgiveness. I was really having a hard time figuring him out. Sometimes he looked like he loved me and at other times he looked like he would have loved to kill me. I pushed him off of me and walked toward the door. I opened the door to leave but he was so tall he reached over my head and slammed it shut.

"I'm sorry for the way I made you feel, but I don't want anything to happen to us. We got a good thing going here. I don't want to stop doing the shows."

The way he made me feel … if he had any idea of what I felt he would have run for his life! I felt like killing him but I didn't want to be a murderer. I hated him at that moment and I hated being with him. I dreaded going home. He made me feel terrible about myself. He challenged everything I said and did; and, he always compared me to someone else, anyone else. At times I felt he made up people to compare me to and he always found something to dislike about the way I was dressed or looked. He made me feel like I was a nameless, faceless old bag just hanging around waiting for him to fill me up with his insults. He made me feel like every woman in the world was beautiful except me. He made me hate him and myself. The way you make me feel is homicidal!

He didn't want us to be together, he just didn't want to stop doing the shows. He constantly told me I thought I was better than he or somehow so different from everyone else. I found myself wondering, on a daily basis, what the heck was wrong with having goals and trying to reach them and why should I want to be like everyone else? He had a way of wrecking my self-confidence and I was beginning to hate him for it. I don't think he really knew how much his badgering got to me. No matter what I did, it was too much or not enough. I wanted out! Out of that Men's Room, out of the marriage and I wanted him completely out of my life. I just wanted out.

Again, I opened the door to leave. This time he didn't try to stop me from opening it but he did grab my arm. He knew it was important to me to be fair … not to jump to unsubstantiated conclusions.

"You know you have no proof. Blascey and I, both, told you that we didn't do anything. You are jumping to a conclusion that you can't prove and you're making me lose my wife, home and livelihood because of an assumption." He stopped for a minute and tried to muster up a tear but it wouldn't come so he continued, "You see I'm here. I didn't go with them. If she was so important to me I would have gone with them and dealt with you tonight. But, I'm here. I don't want to stop doing the shows. We're making a lot of money and we're the best-known troupe in the city! I like Emceeing. You taught me how to do that. I didn't know anything about giving shows before I met you."

I could not believe my ears. There was nothing in his plea for me.   He loved being in front of an audience and he wanted the money. He wanted to continue to do the shows. It gave him something he didn't have, the illusion of a personality and the money to finance the illusion.

I couldn't help remembering the times when the shows weren't successful, the times when we only had a few people in the audience. He didn't want anything to do with the shows in those days. In fact, according to him, I was silly for continuing to do them … to work so hard putting them on for the one or two people who showed up. He didn't want his name associated with it in any way, manner or form back then.   Despite his persistent protests, the models and I kept doing the shows. We did mall shows, tearoom fashion shows, hosting, and demonstrations until almost all fashion events held in Cleveland had a Panache model involved in it. We canvassed the city a few weeks before the shows. We went to all of the hot spots to put flyers on cars. We went to other fashion shows and handed out flyers, and we hired college students to go to the malls to hand out flyers. I did a lot of television and radio talk shows to get more advertisement. We did all of the grunt work that went with getting our troupe's name out there. All of a sudden we had nothing but sold out shows and the people I met started telling me they had met the owner, Jerry! He, who wanted nothing to do with the shows, suddenly owned the business. I didn't ever deny he was the owner because he was my husband and my husband was half owner. He certainly was not the half that worked to build the business but, legally; he owned half of the business. Every time anyone mentioned they had met the owner I felt like I had just been punched in the stomach. I felt like telling them the truth. I wanted to tell them that his part was to show up for the show and disrupt the routines we had established and then showboat the entire time that we were on stage. I wanted to tell them to tell him they knew the truth and not to waste his breath in the future. I knew they had no idea of how things really worked with us, they were going by what they were told and I allowed the lie to stand as the truth because I didn't say anything to counter his claim.

My response was always the same.

"Oh, well, it's nice to meet you. My name is Sarissa Brown and I am the other half of the business."

I'd hold a pleasant conversation with them for a few minutes, invite them to the next show, get some data like a phone number so I, or someone from the troupe, could call them and tell them that we were expecting to see them at the upcoming show and to invite them to our cast party. This was always good public relations and it was one of the reasons that we had such a loyal following. Each time, as I walked away all I could think of was the amount of work that the models and I had put into Panache and it was Jerry who was now walking away with the credit for pulling it all together.

CHAPTER FIVE

I walked back into the rehearsal hall oblivious to everything that was going on. I sat there unable to concentrate. Was I crazy? Did I imagine the wolf? Could something like this really happen to a person like me? After all, I'm the most rational person I know...I'm not prone to nonsense or fantasy! Where was the wolf when I needed him tonight? Why didn't he tear Jerry, Blascey and even Robert apart? Why did those two guys run when they got close to me ... could I have imagined this whole thing?

I had a million questions running through my mind. The only thing I knew for sure was that this was not something I would be able to talk about with anybody but Aleena. Whomever else I would tell something like this to would probably have me committed to Fairhill Mental Hospital. When I snapped out of my fog and my mind was able to focus on the activities taking place, only three models were waiting to be auditioned. The models had done a superb job of getting people in and out and I had spent much more time in that Men's Room with Jerry than I thought. I was excited at the thought of getting the rehearsal over. I would be able to go home and work on summoning the wolf.

I had it all planned. I'd summons the wolf and wait for Jerry to walk through the door. I would scare the living heck out of him by slashing his face with my long, sharp claws. Then I'd back him into the wall and would not allow him to move. I would snarl my snout to make sure he saw how long and sharp my teeth were and then I would back away from him. While he stood there afraid to move, I would transform into myself again and tear up his clothes and everything else he felt was valuable. Then I'd throw all of his stuff out the window. I would watch him stand there helpless to do anything about it and I would dare him to speak. That would be perfect. Jerry would get a taste of his own medicine. He would feel helpless, have no say-so or input, and he would stand and take whatever I dished out. I wondered if I would be able to speak as the wolf. I wanted to say things that would hurt his feelings and fill him with self-doubt. I could not wait; I wanted to get home early so I could figure out how to summons the wolf.

I was so consumed with the wolf that I missed the audition of two of the three remaining people. I looked up to see one of the most breathtakingly beautiful women on the face of this earth standing in the center of the floor. Her name was Anaghia and she was a Native America Indian. That night several multi-nationals had auditioned and were accepted into the group. That was also the night I decided to change the name of the group from Panache Models to the Panache Multi-National Models. The men were as beautiful as the women but most of them had a strong, dominating presence unlike the feeling you get from a beautiful woman. There was Amjad from Pakistan, Mohammed from Israel, Myako from Japan, Anita from Bangladesh, Kenja from Sudan, Nelly from Russia, Lisa from Italy, and Anaghia from South Dakota. The most exotic person to audition was from South Dakota. What kind of nonsense was that? That made me think about all of the people who lived in America and how the Native American Indian was the one who seemed to be the most rare and exotic. I entertained the plight of the Indian people in America and that filled my heart with a deep sorrow that I had never felt before.

For some strange reason, I was consumed with which advertising had brought such a diverse group to us. We had posters, flyers and ads in a variety of magazines and local papers. I resolved to look at the applications to see just where they had heard about Panache. My mind kept jumping from the wolf to the diversity of America and how the Native American was like the foreigner. I thought so deeply about those things that I missed Anaghia's audition.

Anaghia knew I had not paid attention to her audition so she stood in the center of the room and refused to move until I did look at her. Sophie was at the Callback table motioning for Anaghia to come over and get signed up for a callback. Anaghia refused to move. I looked up to see her standing in the center of the room and Sophie motioning to her.

"Sophie is calling you."

She dismissed my statement and asked, "Did you see the movements of the wolf?"

I could not believe my ears. I knew I must have misunderstood her. I shook my head and rubbed my eyes as though I needed to wake up.

"I beg your pardon, what did you say?"

She stood self-assured and very confident. Her words resounded in my ears as she repeated her question, "Did you see the movements of the wolf?"

I became fearful and wanted to run screaming out of the room. I actually gave grave consideration as to whether or not I should run. The idea of answering Anaghia's question with such a reaction was unappealing so I sat there, dazed and, again, trapped like a caged animal - unable to escape. I realized I was not afraid of her...I was afraid I had gone completely crazy and I was now hearing things! I stood slowly and walked over to her so I could watch her mouth as she spoke. I needed to hear exactly what she had to say without any misinterpretations. I was afraid and curious and I could not afford to have any misunderstanding about what I was hearing.

"The external are representative of the internal forces. Fearless, deliberate, focused, forceful, free and fluid... those are the movements of the wolf and that is the way I modeled for you tonight. I moved with the power and the presence of the wolf. The wolf protects my people."

My feet were stuck to the floor or I believe I would have run. I know I wanted to scream and run without stopping but, again, I would have to explain my reaction to the models and I was not ready to share that experience with anyone yet. I moved two steps back from her and then I froze in my tracks, again.

"You, too, move with the power of the wolf, like my people. You know it and so do I."

I stood there, shaking inside, nervous and anxious, wondering if the snout was showing but if this time I was the one who could not see it. I wondered what she knew or could see in me. I certainly didn't see a snout on her but at that point I was looking down at my feet so I wouldn't have to look at her.

For reasons I didn't know, my head lifted up and my eyes looked directly into her eyes. I didn't want this to happen and I could not stop it from happening. In the next instance I was hearing a small, soft voice in my head.

"Look at me. Look into my eyes when I speak to you. You must learn to confront your fears."

I could not stop looking into her eyes. I was screaming in my mind, "Let me get the heck out of here. Let me go, let me go. I want to go."

"Shut up and listen to me. You are under my control; you will do as I say."

Instantly I became irritated at the thought of having someone else controlling my life. I thought... Well, hell, don't this just beat all.

The small soft voice replied, "Yes, it really does but not in the manner that you think. Relax, it will be good for you."

I kept telling myself to shut up over and over in my head and suddenly my voice was silenced, all together. I could not even think a private thought.

"You were getting on my nerves with your chattering. I need your silence and your attention. I am going to release you to move but you must act naturally."

She was in control of my thoughts and movements and I didn't have a thing to say about it.

Anaghia released her hold on me and I was able to speak after a few minutes. Still, her comment about the movement of the wolf lingered heavily in my mind. I didn't know if that was a cultural thing with her - imitating the movements of the wolf - or if she was trying to pique my interest so I would talk about my recent experiences. Either she had some strange powers or else I was hallucinating like nobody's business that day. I sighed with relief when I remembered taking martial arts years ago and some of the strange routines we practiced. We imitated many animals and insects as a part of the cultural beliefs of the Japanese, Korean and Taiwanese people. I thought immediately that copying the movements of the wolf had to be a cultural thing for Native American Indians.

I glanced over at the Callback table and before I knew it Sophie was standing next to me. She gave Josephine one of those get over here quick looks and within seconds Josephine was on the other side of me. James took Anaghia's hand to lead her to the Callback table but she refused to move. James snatched his hand away as if he had just touched fire. Anaghia had a staunch, firm look on her face and she didn't take her eyes off of me.   Stephen stood guard at the door like a British sentry guarding the palace.

As though she was giving me one last chance to come clean, Anaghia asked again..."Did you see the movements and the power of the wolf in my technique? You, too, have the movements and the power of the wolf in you. That's why I am here, because you have become aware of the power of the wolf and it is time that you know why you have that power! You have been made free, your actions and movements are now deliberate and directed. Your movements are in concert with the spirit of canis. You are aware of the wolf, I am sure of it!"

I felt like jumping up out of my chair, running and screaming out the rehearsal hall. Instead, I sat quietly. I searched her face for a snout, long, sharp teeth or yellow orbs. I looked at her intensely but did see anything slightly resembling a wolf.

"I must apologize to you; I always leave the selection process to the models so I was deep in thought when you modeled. If you don't mind, would you repeat your performance?"

She looked into my eyes without answering. She turned and looked at Sophie, Josephine and James as if to say, MOVE! Sophie looked at me first then she defiantly looked into Anaghia's eyes. She held her gaze for about a minute and then she turned her head slowly in alignment with her right shoulder, she threw her shoulders back, stretched her neck up as straight as an arrow, slowly turned her head straight ahead and locked her eyes on the Callback table. She took the most calculated, fluid steps back to the Callback table I had ever seen. When she reached her chair, she did a double pivot from left to right and right to left and sat down flawlessly with perfect posture. I covered my mouth and giggled to myself. I could not stop smiling because that was some of the best modeling I had ever seen her do and she was already an outstanding model. Anaghia smiled with her eyes, mouth and body movement as she clapped for Sophie. Then she bowed to her as though giving homage to a queen. Sophie's expression was staunch, unchanged and uninterested but there was a twinkle in her eyes that shouted, I AM PANACHE...no one comes to Panache Models but through me! Before I knew it everyone in the room was clapping. Sophie never smiled or acknowledged the applause. Her eyes scanned the paperwork on the table and without looking up she motioned for Anaghia to begin her performance.

Anaghia stretched her hand out toward Sophie and lifted her arm as though she had the power to lift Sophie's head and make her look at her. Sophie's head did, in fact, lift in unison with Anaghia's arm and her large, brown eyes were fixed on Anaghia. With everyone's eyes on her, Anaghia began her routine.

She lowered her head and locked her gaze on me. I wanted to look away but I could not. It was as though she had taken control over me and was directing the movement of my eyes. I watched as her right shoulder lowered and her left raised up and moved forward. At the same time her body shifted to the right and forward. Her movements at first glance were graceful and fluid. In the next instance I realized they were slight but directed. She lifted to her tiptoes, moved her left leg back about half a foot so her right foot was in position to step out. Instead of leading with her right foot to move forward she pivoted into a half turn to acknowledge Sophie. Her body was long, rigid and straight but it appeared to be flexible and soft. Her posture was magnificent. Her movements were mesmerizing. She was full of grace and excitement. Her head moved from side to side in acknowledgment of everyone in the room. Then she moved forward as though she had been lifted and was walking on air. She appeared confident, in control, directed. She moved like a mild summer breeze that gently blew past me. Her hair was long and dark and shined like black gold. It was thick and heavy and moved gently from side to side as she moved. Her skin was like brushed gold and had hints of bruised peaches bursting through as though the sun's light was delicately dancing on her, making her glow like an angel.

As I watched her walk I began to see the precision in her movement. Her right hand and left leg and left hand and right leg were moving in perfect harmony reaching forward and back, forward and back, forward and back in directed, precise movements. Her shoulders moved deliberately but very slightly...in concert with her legs. I felt like I was in a trance and could not move my eyes away from her. I felt her movements in my body as I watched and experienced her saunter forward in perfect unison to a four/four beat. I experienced her thoughts as she planned her upcoming movements. There was no movement that wasn't planned and no movement that appeared to be planned. It was like watching, as well as being, a master model skilled at making the art of showmanship and movement effortless. Still on her tiptoes, she covered the entire room, acknowledged each person and showed every piece of clothing that Sophie described. And, as though she had never left that spot, she again was in front of me flawlessly flaunting and twirling on the tips of her toes.

As she lowered herself to the ground she slowly moved her head back so her face was looking up at the ceiling. She placed her left leg about a half a foot behind her right and pivoted into a half turn to acknowledge Sophie. Then she placed her right foot about half a foot in front of her left, raised her arms slowly into the air and did a mannequin turn as she again acknowledged each person in the room. As she completed her performance she slowly lowered her arms and herself to the floor. She was as graceful as a prima ballerina, as precise as a physician, and as colorful and creative as an artist. That rehearsal hall was her canvass, on it; she painted a different picture for each person to see. She enjoined our experiences with hers and moved us with her every step. Her hand movements were a major part of her performance. She placed her hands together; her fingers were straight, pointing down and her elbows aligned perfectly. She artfully turned her hands so they pointed up instead of down. She brought her hands, still clasped together, up to eye level and slowly pulled them apart, gently brushing past her eyes and ears until her arms were lowered to her sides. I was transfixed. She had enslaved me with her eyes and movements. She held me by her will and took over my thoughts. I could not break loose from her grip. I felt like I was in the twilight zone watching a movie where I was sitting in a chair but only capable of entertaining the thoughts she placed in my head. In fact, that is exactly what was going on. Her thoughts overpowered my own and there was nothing I could do. At that point, I really didn't have a thought of my own. Again, she raised her arms above her head; her hands were still together and very, very slowly she lowered her head. Her eyes still fixed on me - she was looking at and through me, her arms moved slowly apart and down until they rested at her side. She moved her right leg far behind her left and took a bow.

Although I stood perfectly still, I had seen the things she had been seeing and experienced her emotions as she moved throughout the room. I was inside of her, looking out – just as I had been with the wolf. I was one with her spirit. In a flash I stopped seeing the grace and showmanship I was accustomed to searching for in a model and I was experiencing the emotions of an animal establishing dominance, taking control, staking out a territory, bringing others into submission and granting permission to be gazed upon by those present. Every movement was used to establish position and leadership and she, definitely, had taken control and had demonstrated she was the dominant force in the room.

When she finally released my thoughts and eyes, I tried to keep my eyes on her because I didn't want anyone else to see I had come under her control. I had a plastic smile that stayed on my face the entire time she modeled. It was a smile I had put on so often it had become a natural part of my routine. I wanted to run out of the room and I wanted to scream, what did you just do to me? I am sure she was aware of my intense desire to run because when I attempted to move I could not...my body was stiff and immovable. My arms and legs felt like each one was a two-ton weight, yet not by my own will, my legs moved me to the center of the room until I was standing face to face with Anaghia. I was being drawn in by her and could not resist. She could read my mind and speak to me without words. I was not afraid of her but I resented the thought of trading one controlling person for another.

"No, it will not be the same. I am here to help free you." The voice was so loud and clear this time I assumed everyone in the room heard it. I was about to speak but again, she spoke to me telepathically. "Do not speak. You are the only one who can hear me."

I nodded in agreement, which was the only thing I could do. I had no control over my actions, movements, thoughts or speech. In the next second I heard myself congratulating her on her excellent style of modeling. Still, I doubted the reality of what had just happened. This experience was difficult for me to rationalize. It was not unusual for me to experience what others experienced but this was the first time I was able to translate the experience into animal instincts and motive.

From early childhood I experienced the same emotions that others experienced. I always assumed I had these experiences because I am such an empathetic person. I felt other people's pain so real and so deeply I have been left with marks on my body. And, I have experienced such euphoric pleasure I was unable to move or speak at the description of another person's experience or touch.

CHAPTER SIX

I sent the models home. They fought me on it but I insisted they leave anyway. Anaghia was waiting to talk with me.

In my mind I said, "I really would like to know more about the wolf. It is a beautiful animal - powerful and fearless - and I like the feeling I had when it was with me." But, in my natural voice I told her I'd see her at our next rehearsal and speak with her at that time.

She smiled and left with the rest of the models. I turned on the video to record Lillian and Andrew. As we sat there talking, the camcorder recorded us. I moved to the edge of the table so that the recorder could get a good picture of them. I had them sit on both sides of the table. I, again, asked why they waited so long to say anything to me.

Lillian said, "I guess cuz we shy."

"You know being shy is one thing but the way you two acted tonight was very strange. You saw everyone's reactions didn't you?"

They began to act like children who were being scolded. They lowered their heads, poked out their bottom lips and jerked back as though I was about to hit them.

I was trying to understand why they were really there. Were they there to get even with me for not speaking to them for ten years? I wanted to know exactly when Lillian had gone into Fair Hill, and under what conditions they had let her out on that day. I didn't want to open up that can of worms so I didn't say anything else about it. I wondered if they understood the point I tried to make when I told them I was shy. I could not imagine anybody thinking of me as being snobbish.

I asked, "Why tonight?"

Andrew said, "It's my birthday. I'm eighteen years old and I wanted to do something special on my birthday."

"So how did you celebrate your birthday?"

"We came here, saw some real models, and we talked to you."

I saw this was not going to get any better so I said, "Okay, let me see what you can do. You first Lillian."

Lillian walked back and forth with the biggest, craziest grin on her face I had ever seen. She had good movements but her turns were very stiff and choppy and she didn't know what to do with her hands. Andrew moved like a machine, stiff and controlled. I showed them how to relax and move at a comfortable pace. I had them talk into the camera, giving me their birth dates, home addresses, social security numbers and a referral. They were both very excited and gave me all of the information I requested. I told them I was concerned about them joining the group and I needed their parents' consent. They insisted they were old enough so I had them show me their ID to prove they were at least eighteen years old. They both showed me their drivers' license. It wasn't Andrew's birthday. He was twenty-eight, not eighteen. And the address he had given me was incorrect.

I gave them both an application to fill out.

Lillian asked, "Do we come to the next rehearsal?"

"Yes, us shy people have got to stick together."

Lillian hugged my neck so tight her little bony arms felt like a rope around my throat. I felt myself begin to lose consciousness. I felt faint and dizzy, almost unable to stand. My footing was unsure and my balance was off centered. It felt like the room was spinning around me. I knew any second I'd be falling to the ground. For some reason, my legs were stiff and still. It was then I realized I was trying desperately to allow myself to fall prey to a villainous act that would bring the wolf back to me again. I also realized how strong my desire was to see or be the wolf again. In my mind, I had experienced weakness, dizziness and the room spinning. If none of those things had occurred how could I be sure I had truly experienced the wolf? I wondered if my mind could have been playing tricks on me then, too. Could I have needed an escape from my life so badly I created a strong, ferocious animal to be my hero – and better yet, an animal from within me? How pathetic, how absolutely pathetic, I thought.

What about the two men who ran from me tonight and what about Anaghia? There had to be something to it! I could not have been imagining this; at least I prayed I wasn't imagining it!

I closed and opened my eyes several times, almost automatically. Actually, I bordered on being unable to stop. Finally, I opened my eyes and took a deep breath only to find I was not about to black out. Disappointed, I stood there - numb, unable to muster a reaction to Lillian's show of affection. Instead of hugging her I was filled with rage. I slowly raised my right hand and firmly gripped the small of her elbow that rested on my left shoulder. As I held her elbow, my teeth clenched together and my jaws seemed to pull back and lock. I could feel the nerve endings in my face jump to the beat of my heart. I must have squeezed her elbow for at least fifteen seconds. I didn't think about Lillian or that I might have inadvertently been hurting her. Instead I thought of my inability to summons the wolf and experience that feeling of freedom and strength that came with it. With that thought I became more disappointed. I squeezed her elbow with an unyielding force and abruptly pulled her long skinny arm from around my neck. She took a step back and looked deep into my eyes. It was as if she thought she would find an answer for why I had just hurt her. I had never been purposefully mean to any person before. But I was becoming filled with rage and I wanted to physically hurt something or even someone. She just happened to be the closest one to me at the time. But, she would never find a rational reason for what I had just done because I didn't have one.

Andrew stood there with a strange, bewildered look on his face. They looked at each other and smiled. I looked at Lillian and she had a huge smile that spread from one end of her face to the other and her eyes were wide and wild with excitement. She looked like a raving lunatic. It was quite distasteful; I could see all of her teeth, her fillings and her gums. "Yuck," is the only word I could think of to describe that smile.

Andrew moved out of my line of sight to my side but I could still see every move he made with my peripheral vision. I could see his right hand move slowly down deep into his pants pocket.

"Finally," I said in a soft, low voice, "some semblance of danger! Surely, the wolf will come back to me now."

Lillian turned almost in slow motion to Andrew; she started shaking her head, yes. He copied her and they stood there like two lunatics shaking their heads up and down with huge disturbing smiles on their faces. I wanted to be afraid but I was angry at the lunacy that was going on. Suddenly, I heard the loud clatter of the doors bursting open and a table and chair being knocked over. I turned to see who had come through the door and it was Sophie, Josephine, James and Stephen. Sophie walked up and grabbed Andrew's hand to pull it out of his pocket. He had a long hatpin with a cap on the end of it.

Sophie screamed out in anger at me, "I am so damn mad at you." She balled her fist up like she was going to punch Andrew and said, "And you...you ... what were you going to do with this pin? Boy, do you know I will hurt..." then she bit her lip and didn't complete the sentence.

My eyes were as wide as theirs at that point because I could not believe none of them trusted my judgment in being left alone with Lillian and Andrew. I couldn't believe she was mad at me when I was the one who should have been mad at them. Stephen walked up to Andrew and whispered something in his ear. Andrew stood there mortified and wet himself. I asked what he had said but neither spoke. Andrew tried to speak but no words would come out. Lillian still had that crazy smile on her face. She sat down in the middle of the floor and started punching herself in the arm.

"They ain't gonna like this, they gonna be mad. They ain't gonna like this, they gonna be mad."

I had to admit I really didn't, in my heart of hearts, think I was alone with those two. I knew Sophie had to go and see about her kids but I figured James and Stephen would still be somewhere in the area. Andrew stood there with tears flowing from his large eyes. Then he cried out..."We only loved you. That's all we did. But you just hated us cause we po." Then he fell to the ground and laid there with his face pressed to the floor and his arms crossed over the back of his head.

I felt so bad I wanted to cry. I apologized profusely over and over and promised to personally train them and make sure they became a part of the Panache Models organization. Sophie looked at me and rolled her eyes. She was so angry I began to choke. It was the strangest thing. I could feel her anger and her hands around my throat even though she stood more than a yard away from me.

I could barely choke out the words, "Sophie, stop…stop choking me."

She stepped back in disbelief. She ran up to me and hugged me but then she jumped away from me in fear. She apologized and told me that at that moment she had been visualizing choking me. She said she was choking me so hard in her mind she could feel my neck in her hands. My eyes were red and burning and my neck was red and purple as if I had just been choked. She was really frightened and started walking backwards. She was pointing to my neck.

"What's going on with you? What's happening to you?" she asked as she backed away. "Your neck is red just like somebody has been choking you!"

Josephine started screaming..."What? What? What is it Sophie? Why did you choke her?"

Josephine started running toward me but Sophie turned to her and pulled her away before she got too close.   "That's what I'm talking about. I just thought about choking her but I never got close enough to touch her and just look at her neck!"

Josephine ran to the door and started screaming. She ran out into the hallway and back into the rehearsal hall.

"Well how in the hell did her neck turn red like she been choked?"

I said "Because Lillian's skinny little arms were wrapped around my neck so tight that my neck was bruised and burned."

James sat down and said, "That explains it so can we go now?"

Everyone was relieved.

Andrew still lay on the floor with his arms crossed over his head and burying his face into the floor. I assumed he was just so ashamed he didn't know what else to do. I felt humiliated and ashamed for him. I needed to clean up the mess he left before I could lock the room. I asked everyone in the room to swear this incident would never be talked about again. Everyone agreed. Stephen bent down next to Andrew and whispered something in his ear. Andrew looked up at Stephen and reached out his hand. Stephen pulled him to his feet and walked with him to the Men's Room. He came back into the rehearsal hall and held up his hand. He had the spare key to my apartment. It was clenched between his thumb and index finger. Sophie must have given it to him. I looked at him and then looked for Andrew. He pointed down the hall to the Men's Room. Again, he held his hand up with the key pressed in the middle of his palm to ask if it was okay to go to my apartment. This time, I shook my head, yes. Stephen went to my apartment and got my hair dryer. I didn't know what he had said to Andrew, but whatever it was...Andrew seemed to be okay with it. When they got back from the Men's Room, Andrew stood at the door and called for Lillian to join him. Stephen walked them to their car. By the time Stephen got back to the rehearsal hall we had cleaned up the urine and had put the chairs back in place.

Even though I lived in the building I went for a ride with Sophie and Josephine. That was a safety precaution we took just in case anyone who had auditioned was hanging around. We instituted that policy when we first got together but this time with Lillian and Andrew being so set on finding out where I lived it suddenly made sense. After all, Lillian had just gotten out of a hospital for the mentally ill and Andrew acted like he had been there too.

CHAPTER SEVEN

I remembered, briefly, an experience I had with an old boyfriend. His name was Lester and he was wild and crazy. He scared me because he experimented with drugs. Someone must have dropped him off at Marymount Hospital on that particular day. In his condition he could not have driven himself. Lester, as was his habit of the previous year, had taken some bad drugs and was in a comatose state. He could not speak. Crystal Venable, one of my friends, was there to see her mother. While there, she saw Lester on a gurney in the hallway. She heard two doctors talk about him so she gave them my name and number. The doctors couldn't make heads or tails out of Lester's situation so they called me. I couldn't answer any of their questions over the phone because I didn't know what was going on. They asked me to come in to see if I could evoke some type of reaction out of him. I thought about telling his father so he could go and see about him but they were like fire and ice when they were together. Mr. Aucchon would probably cause more harm than good. I decided to make the decision on whether or not to get Mr. Aucchon involved after I had a chance to see Lester. When I got there he still could not talk. The doctors told me, then, he was comatose. If they had told me before, I surely would have told his father so he could see about him. The doctors didn't know what he had taken so they really didn't know what to do for him.

Lester and I were very close and there were times I felt I knew exactly what he wanted me to know just by touching him. As I stood there helpless to do anything about his situation, I prayed silently and asked God to help me help him or at least get some kind of reaction out of him. I was about to rub his hair to comfort him. My habit was to run my finger across his eyebrows first and then rub his hair. As soon as my finger touched his eyebrow a sea of colors blinded me. The colors were vivid and fluid. They moved like strikes of lightening through my head. As soon as a color became apparent to me, like a burst of red, it would then explode into a multitude of colors and flow into a new and different one. This explosion of colors shocked me and I immediately started to move away but he lifted his hand up toward me. As soon as I touched the tips of his fingers I immediately began to describe his experiences.

My hand, throat, and head started burning like fire and throbbing as though something inside of me was banging and banging trying to get out. I tried to back away from him because the experience was so painful but by that time Lester had a good grip on my hand and he was squeezing it. The heat from his hand penetrated my skin and ran rampant through my body. It started in the hand he held so tightly. My fingers burned like fire and pulsated from his rapid and intense heartbeat. Within seconds a fiery, burning energy raced up through my hand to my arms, shoulders, and neck and then into my head. It was a scorching hot sensation that burned inside of my veins like acid. When it reached my head it felt like I had been dunked in a vat of fire. It burned my eyes, ears and nose and the cavities that connected each. I remembered thinking if I had touched my skin, it might have burned and peeled right off. The burning was pervasive in my head and neck area and it seemed to swelter and swirl around that area longer than any other. As soon as the heat reached my shoulder area it quickly moved back down into my mid section and then down through my hips, thighs, legs and feet. My bones were burning and my insides felt like they were boiling. After reaching the tips of my toes the burning quelled and left the lower part of my body. It stayed in my head a few minutes longer. The burning feeling was now restricted to my head and neck. My head was pounding and my eyes felt like they were about to burst open.

I felt like I was about to black out. My legs got weak and my body wavered as though I was going to fall. At first the doctors stood there looking at me like they didn't know what to do or whether they should believe me. My eyes were fire red and my nose started bleeding so they knew they had to do something. One of the doctors shoved a thermometer in my mouth. My temperature had shot up to 101 degrees and I was instantly filled with fever. My throat was scratchy and burning and it hurt when I opened my mouth. The cold air felt like it was cutting my raw, red throat into pieces. The more I spoke, the more it hurt me to speak. The doctors insisted what I described was not possible for me to experience just by taking his hand. Lester squeezed my hand tighter and strangely enough, my head and neck stopped hurting.

In the next few seconds I was watching him walk into a room with a blood stained red door. Behind the door were three girls and another man. Each of them was sitting on the floor around a huge wood-framed table with a glass top.   Strewn across the table were a few tubes of model airplane glue, some LSD, six empty wine bottles, a half-filled bottle of grape wine and a pile of green and white pills. He sat down and took a big gulp from the bottle of wine, and then he took the paper bag with the glue in it from one of the girls, clasped it round his mouth and nose and started inhaling so deeply that his heart felt like it was going to burst. He took the bottle the man had and lit one of the strange looking purple pipes that were attached to the long tube extending from the bottle and smoked some marijuana. He stopped for a minute and gave the man a very strange and odd look. The marijuana had been mixed with something that was unfamiliar to him. After a few seconds he put the pipe back into his mouth and inhaled longer and deeper than he had before. One of the girls pulled a needle out of her arm.

"You got to try this out ...it's out of this world, for real...if it don't kill you, you'll never be able to get this high again."

He stuck his hand out and she stuck the needle in between his fingers. Then he took a small blue tab of LSD and put it under his tongue. His skin started turning yellow, white and red. His body started shaking and he started getting chest pains. He could not breathe.

I felt the stabbing pains in my chest and started gasping for air. My eyes started to burn and water when one of the doctors broke Lester's grip on my hand. I began to feel better but I could not move or breathe normally. Normal breathing felt like a jagged dagger in my heart and any movement felt like leather straps tightening around my chest. One doctor attended to me and gave me some kind of shot.

I heard the other doctor yell out, "Needle mark between his ring and middle finger on his left hand."

They rushed him into the back room and started working on him. It was a short time before he walked out of the room. I hadn't thought about that experience for years, until that day. Somehow I had been inside of him and felt everything he felt...just like that night, when I felt everything that Anaghia felt and experienced her every thought!

Finally, I snapped out of my spell-like journey into the past and looked around the room to see everyone's reaction. I wanted to make sure that no one was looking at me and gauging my reaction to Anaghia. I was not sure of how much time I had spent going through that memory nor was I sure of what I was doing while I was going through it. I couldn't bear the thought of sitting there and reacting to something that nobody else could see; or, was even aware of. That was the last thing I needed to worry about. I looked around but no one seemed to be paying any attention to me at all. I guessed that everyone was still spinning from his or her own experience with Anaghia. Sophie was the least affected but she was affected nonetheless. Still, she stood up and bowed to Anaghia. Josephine was jumping up and down clapping, and then she composed herself.

"She completes our troupe...after tonight we should not do any more recruiting. We will be messing with perfection if we do."

James was wiping the sweat off of his brow. His body was wrapped around his chair with one leg stuck in between the top and bottom pads. I could not imagine what he had done to get tangled up in that chair. His shirt was wet and he was taking long, deep, deliberate breaths, almost panting. That was either the strangest reaction I had ever seen or James has just gone straight.

Stephen was no longer standing at attention at the door; he had his hands in his pocket and was doing mannequin turns on his toes like Anaghia. I also noticed that whenever he turned he would fan himself. His eyes were fixed looking up, as though he was in the midst of the most erotic pleasure imaginable.

I stared into Anaghia's eyes as I spoke. "I saw the movements that you spoke of and they were beautiful."

"Yes it is beautiful, and powerful, to know the wolf."

Still, uncertain of what I had just experienced, and myself I asked, "Is that something that you practice a lot... the movements of the wolf?"

In my mind I pleaded with her for understanding since I had had strange experiences my entire life that no one else seemed to be able to tap into. I felt she could hear my thoughts but I could not be certain. I was not certain whether my mind had taken me on a trip as she performed or if it was she who created and controlled those experiences.

"I do understand your hesitation and fears." Still, she looked extremely disappointed. She added, "You don't practice, you embrace."

"I'm confused. I think you are saying something more to me than it appears."

"I am telling you I, too, know the wolf," she said in a soft, compassionate voice.

At this point, I was more rattled than confused. I was not sure of when she was speaking to me aloud or in my mind. I persisted in my same vein of rejecting her theory of the wolf.

"Okay."

In my mind I began to doubt the experience and I tried to shrug it off as some Indian cultural thing. I began to turn away from her because I feared she would touch me and I would then experience her feelings on a much deeper level. I moved back and turned to move away from her.

She then spoke to me telepathically again. "The feelings you had were real. You were one with me, one with my spirit. I am your shaman. I will reveal all that you need to know. You will come to understand more and I will lead you. You are a part of my family, the family of canis. You must come to know who you are and the powers that you have."

Again, I looked around the room to see how many people heard her. No one seemed to be confused by what she had just said so I assumed she had spoken to me, telepathically, again. Again, in my mind, I begged her to spare me the experience. I was confused and I felt I would be answering her aloud when she was speaking to me telepathically. I didn't want the models to think I was losing my mind because, at that point, I felt that losing my mind was a real possibility. I tried not to think about the fact I really didn't want her in the troupe because I was fearful of what I would learn or I would become more focused on the wolf and neglect Panache. But, Anaghia would make a beautiful addition to our troupe and that meant a lot to the other models. The thought that Anaghia would be the most beautiful model in the city of Cleveland and she would be a Panache Model turned my plastic smile into a genuine feeling of happiness, and with that, I smiled bigger and more genuinely than ever.

CHAPTER EIGHT

There were still two people seated. They were not there when I left to go to the Men's Room and I hoped, deep in my heart, they were not there to audition. I really wanted to get home and summons the wolf to greet Jerry. I asked Sophie if they had already auditioned. She told me they didn't want to and that she didn't feel comfortable because they wanted to sit through the auditions and they refused to leave until they talked to me. I asked why she didn't tell me earlier. She rolled her eyes and walked back to the table. I knew exactly what that meant. Let them wait if they didn't want to give her any information. They would sit there and suffer the consequences for not disclosing their business to her. Sophie was as sweet as a Georgia peach but when she was offended, nothing but time would heal that wound. She was going to make them sit and wait until she was ready to introduce them to me.

Even though they really didn't look poised enough to be from another troupe, I still wondered if they were there to spy. As paranoid as that sounds, it was not uncommon for recruiters from other troupes to sneak into our rehearsals to try to recruit our models or to try to get to those who were auditioning for our troupe. One troupe had their trainer audition for us to learn our techniques and routines. I was flabbergasted when I attended their show, saw a number of our routines being performed and heard them introduce Sylvia as their trainer. As was the custom in those days when other models were in the audience, the Emcee would pay some sort of homage by either asking them to stand to be recognized or by calling their names. That night the Emcee made the mistake of calling the Panache Models and another troupe to the stage. I sat in my seat while the models went to the stage. As soon as Sophie hit the stage she grabbed the microphone, described her outfit, asked them to spotlight me and began to tell the story of Panache. Instead of setting the microphone down she handed it off to Stephen, who described his outfit and handed it off to Josephine who described her outfit and motioned for me to come to the stage. I shook my head, No, but the audience at that point was in an uproar. Sophie took the microphone again and talked about the origins of some of the routines that the other troupe had just performed and how Sylvia was not just a trainer for that troupe, she had been coming to our rehearsals as well. She asked me to stand, and I did.

As I stood, the Panache models all posed like mannequins. As Sophie gave out the date of our next show I walked to the edge of the row of seats and posed. The models filed off stage. Before they exited the stage they performed the finale for the routine the troupe was to perform that night. When we left the room, most of the audience left, too. We left the other troupe scrambling for a way to end their show. The Emcee of the show was left with nothing to say. He looked at Sylvia and handed her the microphone. He followed us out the door and asked if he could join our troupe.

I was wondering how much time had elapsed again as I sat there waiting for Sophie to introduce me to the two people. It seemed that my mind was wondering all over the place. I had never been so distracted at a rehearsal before. I looked in their direction. They were sitting next to each other almost at the other end of the rehearsal hall. I didn't want to go over to the other side of the room...not because it was so far away from everyone else, but to establish up front control. I sat at the Callback table with Sophie and motioned for them to come over. The male was a very pretty man, beautiful in fact, but he was extremely thin, almost to the point of being emaciated. He looked anxious and confused. The female was also pretty but a great make-up job would have made her beautiful. She, too, was extremely thin and had the same look on her face - confusion and anxiety. I wondered if they had been using drugs but I was not planning to ask unless they wanted to join the troupe.

The people in our troupe had to take good care of themselves, make logical, good choices, both in their private and public lives and present a good look at all times. If they didn't it would have been easy for anyone to place a label on all of the models based on what one of them had done. Panache was establishing itself and needed to have an impeccable reputation. And, that is exactly what it had, an impeccable reputation!

The two visitors saw me looking at them and they jumped to their feet and ran over to me. That was a strange reaction for two people to have. They were acting like children. They stood next to me on both sides of my chair. They waited until I told them to sit. His name was Andrew. He pulled her chair out for her and then took a seat on the other side of me. Without thinking I patted him on the back because I always liked men who exhibited the traits of a gentleman.

"My name is…"

The woman, Lillian, interrupted me.

"We already know your name. We know a lot about you. You live in this building. Where? I mean you do live here, right? Are you going straight home tonight?"

I was taken aback by her direct questions so I decided to be very direct with my answer and questions.

"I don't tell strangers where I live. Why do you ask?"

Sophie tried to soften the mood; she saw my smile and demeanor had changed from friendly to defensive.

"A lot of people who know her well don't know where she lives." She tried to laugh but stopped abruptly when the woman asked again.

"I just wanted to see if you would tell me where you live and when you gonna be at home tonight. "

I looked into her eyes and answered angrily, "Well, like I said, I don't tell strangers where I live. So, again, why do you ask?"

"I heard you talk about some of the things that you do in your spare time and I know you like to draw so I was going to bring you some art supplies as a gift!"

"That's not a good reason for you to ask where I live when you are sitting here with me right now, now is it? And anyway, when did you ever hear me talk sketching or drawing?"

She started laughing uncontrollably like a crazy person.

"You don't remember saying that? Remember, remember, remember when you used to dance on that show, you said your hobby was art...pen and ink and chalks!"

I could not believe my ears...that had to have been more than ten years ago.

"I used to dance just like you; I still do dance like you, just like you! I can do all of your moves. I'm a dancer, just like you."

"I'm not a dancer. My dancing days ended a long time ago."

Andrew chimed in, "But you still dance, I watch you!"

"No I don't dance professionally ... and did you say you watch me?"

"Yeah! We see you at the clubs but you never speak to us. In ten years, you never did speak to us! We always wanted to be your friend."

Sophie stood up, threw her hands in the air and shouted. "Git out!"

She pointed to the door for them to leave. In a flash, Sophie, Josephine, James and Stephen were at the table. Sophie's veins poked out on her neck when she spoke. "You two must be crazy. Y'all watched her for ten years and now you two are here! What the hell do you want?"

My brother, Toot, was living in Minnesota but the one thing he always told me was not to show any fear to crazy people.

I knew I had to find out something about them. I said, "It's okay, they can stay."

Sophie was angry at my response. "Okay so you are the one that's crazy, not them."

I was just as concerned but I knew I could not show any kind of fear or give them any control. I had to make them think they didn't upset me or get to me. But, hearing that boy or man, whatever he was, say he watched me really shook me up. Andrew folded his arms and rested his head on the table and stared at me.

"I'm sorry I didn't say anything to you. I am very shy with new people. In the ten years you've seen me, you must have noticed I don't meet new people easily."

His body jerked into an upright position.

"Because you're shy?"

"Yes, extremely."

"You ain't shy, you know a lot of people, you speak to groups of people and you go on talk shows, and you always talking to somebody. Yeah, you are always talking to somebody. Remember, I watch you! I see you all the time and people are always coming up to you, talking to you."

"I do a lot of things professionally, not socially. I am very shy. I don't know a lot of people but I do come in contact with quite a few. I have only a few friends. And you just said it yourself; people are always coming up to me. I'm too shy to go up to new people. I don't know how or why I got into this business as shy as I am!"

They looked at each other and smiled insanely with the most disturbing grins I had ever seen.

Lillian jumped out of her seat and sat on the edge of the table. She rocked back and forth as she spoke, "I just can't believe you are shy."

"Why didn't you say anything to me in all of that time?"

"We didn't think you would talk to somebody like us."

"What do you mean, somebody like us? How are you?"

She had a sad, angry look on her face when she said, "Po…po people like us!"

"Girl, you should see where I come from in Youngstown; there is no such thing as 'somebody like us,' in the bad sense. Poor is not a way of life, it is a temporary condition and in some people's lives, it is an attitude. I don't think anybody was poorer financially than my family, but we are rich with love and ambition."

Then I changed the subject.

"So, since you see I will not going to tell you where I live... tell me what I can do for you? Did you want to audition?"

In unison, they both said, "No."

I felt they really wanted to be apart of something like this and I needed a way to get personal information from them so I decided to make them audition.

"Well, since you made me stay here a lot longer than I planned you had better audition. Oh, and, I'm not taking NO for an answer. You both have the bodies...even though you need to eat and put some meat on your bones and you both dance, so why not audition?"

Lillian answered first, "I just don't think I could. I could never get out there in front of people like that!"

I nodded with understanding. "I used to feel that way too! But you get over it. Just imagine you are somebody who goes out there all the time."

Lillian laughed uncontrollably again. "I always do that. I always act like I'm you when I go on the dance floor. And, girl, let me tell you something...I can dance, dance, dance...when I'm you!"

She sat silently, slowly looking me up and down, up and down, up and down.

Finally, I said, "Where did you come from?"

She blurted out, "I just got out of Fair Hill today. You know what Fair Hill is? It's a hospital for the mentally ill. Even though I didn't ever feel ill or sick. You know, like I was gonna throw up or anything."

Sophie blurted out, "I knew a girl who was crazy. She kept laughing like she couldn't stop or like she was on something. It was irritating. I'm telling you it was nerve-racking to be around her." She looked at me and then at both of them and said, "That's it. Y'all git'n the hell out of here now."

I patted her hand and said, "No, it really is okay for them to stay."

She bent down so her face would be level with mine. She looked deep into my eyes, took a deep breath and let out a loud scream that caused me to jerk and almost jump out of my seat. Then she straightened up, rolled her eyes at me and walked to the door. She opened the door and shouted, "You need to just go and check into Fair Hill yo'self 'cause you are acting like you ain't got no sense!" Then she slammed the door.

CHAPTER NINE

It was Wednesday, Lady's night at the Togo Suite. The club was packed to the gills, cars were around the corner and every parking lot in the block was full. We could not find a place to park so we went over to The Reason Why, another upscale club, at Shaker Square. Robert's car was out front so I knew Jerry would be there. Stephen and James pulled up next to us. Stephen motioned for us to roll the window down. I really didn't want to go inside because I didn't want to run into Jerry. Stephen told us the car that Andrew and Lillian had gotten into was there. It was a cute little sports car. I didn't know anything about cars so I didn't know the model or make - all I knew was it was cute and the license plate read "MYTURN".

Sophie pulled off suddenly. I looked back and I could see Jerry walking out of the club with Blascey. I turned to look at Sophie and she had one of those don't start with me, looks on her face.

I said, "I was not about to start with you!"

She hit the brakes so hard and suddenly that Stephen ran into the back of her car. She got out of the car and motioned for Josephine to get out too! I had had enough; I got out of the car and asked her what she was doing.

She said, "You reading my mind, girl!" I was just thinking... "Don't start with me!"

"You always say, don't start with me, when you don't want to be questioned about your actions. I didn't read your mind; I predicted what you would say so I said it first."

Josephine said, "Something is going on with you though and you ain't telling us what it is. You were acting different tonight. Something is different and it isn't the idea of getting rid of Jerry. There is something going on with you! You saw how that Indian girl acted toward you. It was like y'all two were on the same wavelength. I mean, when she looked at me I felt funny and uncomfortable. Like she was looking through me."

"What did her looking at you, have to do with me?"

Josephine just shook her head and shrugged her shoulder. "I don't know, but it had something to do with you and I know it."

Sophie had a sympathetic tone when she spoke, "I know you ain't doing nothing different on purpose but there is something different about you tonight." She let out a long sigh and then continued, "I don't have a bad feeling about you but I have a strange feeling. It's sort of scary. I just can't describe it and I really thought you were reading my mind!" I touched her hand and electricity sparked and shocked both of us. She jerked away from me and screamed. Then she said, "I'm taking you home, we ain't on no carpet for us to be getting shocked. We ain't on no carpet."

As we drove to my apartment Josephine talked the entire time. I was not disinterested in what she had to say but I could not concentrate on it either. She sounded like one of the characters in a Charlie Brown cartoon. You know the ones who talk to Snoopy while he's the Red Baron and all he can hear is background noise like "BLAH, BLAH, BLAH … BLAH, BLAH, BLAH, BLAH … BLAH!"   Well, that was all I heard, it was like background noise that made absolutely no sense at all. It ended up being faded sounds that moved in and out of earshot.

We were in front of my building in no time. It seemed like only a few minutes had passed. The ride back from Shaker Square was at least thirty minutes and if I had to swear how much time it took to get home that night, I'd have to say anywhere between three to five minutes. I got out of the car and walked to the doorway of the building.   I stood at the entrance for a while. My heart was sinking down into my stomach.   I just didn't want to go back to my apartment. Sophie and Josephine got out of the car, ran up to me and hugged me. Stephen and James joined us. The five of us stood at the entrance of the door hugging for about two minutes. I was getting ready to tell them how much I appreciated them being there for me and they all said, in unison…

"I know."

I looked at each of them and said, "This is strange. This time I felt like you all was reading my mind."

Again, in unison, they said, "I felt you."

Josephine screamed, ran back to the car and then back to the entrance where we stood. "This is weird, this is weird...but it's cool if we all got the gift."

I couldn't help smiling when I looked at her. I said, "The gift. That's a good one. I wonder what the gift is?" with that thought I went up to my apartment.

I heard the creaking of my neighbor's door opening as I stood in front of my apartment. Even though he could be seen through the crack in the door, when I looked in his direction I didn't see him or anything. My mind was blank. I don't think I would have seen a MAC truck if it had been sitting there. My mind was somewhere else completely. When I wrapped my hand around the doorknob, a somber, dark feeling came over me. I felt like someone had turned the lights out and had pulled a huge bag over my head. Each breath I took seemed to be heavy, belabored and suffocating. There was a heaviness that moved from the top of my head down through my chest, arms, stomach, legs and feet. My heart felt big and heavy, the darkness that moved through me seemed to temporarily encase me.   It was hard to breath, I felt like a gigantic vice had been clamped around my chest and two hands were closing around my heart - squeezing it, daring it to beat. With each beat, I felt a gripping pain that pierced every piece of my heart and shot throughout the rest of my body like fine slithers of glass fragments. I imagined the chambers of my heart being ripped apart.

I opened the door and walked into a dark, empty apartment. Without turning on any lights I walked into the bedroom. I sat there on the edge of the bed, empty of thoughts and emotions. After a few minutes a sense of calm came over me and I sat quiet and content to be there alone. I sat for hours. I walked over to the window and opened it wide. I stood there looking at the dark sky and breathing in the cold air. It was refreshing. I didn't see the snout and I wasn't looking from within the wolf, but for some reason, I could see much farther than I could

before.   I saw little details that would have been
impossible for me to see a few days earlier. I could clearly
see people inside of their apartments.   I looked up and
down the street in amazement at how much more clearly
and farther I could see.   After my eyes glanced over the
buildings, streets and cars, I looked down to the parking
lot below me. I wanted to make sure I could see things as
well close up as I could far away. When I looked down, I
saw the car Andrew and Lillian had driven to rehearsal. It
was definitely the same car - a cute little sports car with
the license plate that read "MYTURN".   It was parked in
my space in the parking lot.   It was dark inside of the car
but I could see the outlines of two people in the front
seat. I stood there, silent, for at least fifteen minutes. I
turned on the light and after a few minutes there was a
lot of movement in the car or rumbling...and it pulled off
abruptly.

I stood there looking onto the parking lot but my
mind had taken me to another place.   This time I was
watching the pointed tips of a pair of Bruno's - brown
alligator wingtip shoes - as they stepped into the hallway
of my building. I watched the pattern of the floor against

the strip of carpet that led up to the elevator. I saw a finger covered by a pair of black leather rider gloves touch the elevator button. It was Jerry I was watching. What was going on? How could I possibly be looking down at his shoes and see him press the elevator button from the apartment lobby. I was seeing these things as though I were inside of him. I didn't feel anything else. I mean, no emotions, nothing. Suddenly, I felt a surge of negative heat coming from the hallway. It was directed toward me. I knew it was coming from Jerry. I decided to focus on his movement and not his intentions. I wanted to see exactly what he was doing and going to try to do to me. I could see Jerry's shoes as they moved closer to the doorway of my apartment. I watched them as they stopped at the door. I could feel the nervousness in his hand as he tried to steady it so he could grab the doorknob. I felt, and could hear, the long sigh he exhaled as he grabbed the doorknob to open the door. I saw his right hand dig into his pocket and move the long hatpin with the cap on its tip aside so he could get his keys. It was the same hatpin Andrew had and that was the same car Andrew had driven.

I knew instinctively Jerry was going to try to stick me with that pin. Whether it would kill me, paralyze me or just knock me out for a while, I didn't know. I also felt I was being forewarned and protected so I was not afraid. Under any other circumstances I would have cowered down and tried to stay out of Jerry's way. Then I would have sulked the rest of the day because I did nothing to defend myself. But, this time was different, this time I was ready to meet the challenge. Suddenly, I could see the image of Lillian hugging me so tight I'd black out. Andrew would cautiously take the hatpin out of his pants pocket and remove the cap. He would twist the cap to ensure that every bit of the solution was smeared onto the tip before he would stick me. I could also see myself drowsy and unable to speak, being walked out and put into their car. Jerry and Blascey would be waiting. That was as far as I got before this vision disappeared.

The sound of the door opening snapped me back into reality. Jerry stood in the living room in the dark. I didn't move. I sat calmly awaiting his attack and planning mine. He had never attacked me physically, in the past, but this time my senses led me to believe he would.

As he opened the door to the bedroom I said in a soft but demanding voice, "Turn on the light, Jerry."

He turned it on. He had a look of lunacy on his face. He was emotionally distraught, I could see that, but this was more like the craziness that mass murders must experience right before they go on their killing sprees.

Still, unaffected and unafraid, I locked in on his eyes and said, "Empty your pockets."

His eyes opened wide with amazement. His voice was low, scratchy and garbled - as if he had a sore throat - he was almost whispering when he said, "My pockets are empty."

This time my voice became more demanding and unyielding but my tone was even softer than before and I repeated. "Empty your pockets, Jerry!"

His eyes opened wider and wider. It was a terrible sight...his top and bottom eyelids moved away from the center at the same time. Pretty soon all I could see were two big white balls with black circles in them. It was a strange and unappealing sight to see.

"You shouldn't do your eyes like that; it makes you look crazy and unappealing. Just makes you look downright ugly, in fact."

"What, ugly!"

His looks were very important to him so he snapped out of it, looked in the mirror, gave himself one of those big plastic smiles and then he looked at me. A huge smile crept up on his face as he looked at me. It was one of those looks people give to dogs or some other wild animal when they want to calm the animal and back away from it. He nervously walked backward toward the door. He put his hand in his pocket. As his hand entered his pocket I could see him trying to get the hatpin into his glove. He took his keys out and sat them on the dresser. He had a nervous look on his face.

"You didn't get it into your glove! It's still in your pocket," I said in a low, knowing voice.

Jerry screamed, grabbed his keys and ran out the door. He pulled the door shut and held on to it with his entire might. I could hear him fumbling with the key. He was trying to lock the door. I walked over to the bedroom door and put my hand on the knob. I heard his key fall on the floor.

He screamed out, "What the hell has gotten into you? What the hell has gotten into you?"

"Move away from the door, Jerry." I could hear him patting around on the floor for the key with one hand while he tried to keep the door pulled shut with the other. "Move!" I shouted.

He screeched out a high-pitched, "No."

If that situation had not been such a grave one I would have found humor in his reactions. Instead, I was angered at the fact he had plotted against me and was trying to hurt, and possibly, kill me. I still had my hand on the doorknob. I felt him pulling on the opposite side of the door. He was pulling so hard and holding the door so tight the bones and joints in the center of his hands were hurting and his fingers were becoming numb and quickly losing their strength. I could feel his pain.

I twisted the doorknob and snatched the door open in one swift movement. When the door opened, he ran out of the apartment. He was inside the elevator pressing the button as though the door was going to close quicker. I stuck my hand in the doorway to break the infrared connection and the door opened. I made up some crazy hand movement as though I could do magic.

I stretched my head back as far as it could go and I mumbled the words, "Mumble, jumble, humble, Dumbo." On the word Dumbo, I pointed to Jerry.

He screamed and jumped to the back of the elevator. The door didn't open again. I could see Jerry, though. He was walking around in circles inside of the elevator. He put his hand in his pocket and felt the hatpin. He took it out of his pocket and threw it on the floor. I heard the neighbor's door unlatch again and the door crack open. This time the man walked into the hallway. He looked me up and down like he was angry with me and wanted to say something. His cold stare warmed and he held out his arms, again. I would not acknowledge him. I went into my apartment and shut the door. A minute later, I heard a very soft tapping on the door.

Next I heard my neighbor say, "When is your next show. I plan to be there for you."

Without opening the door I said, "I'll pay you not to come."

I sat on my bed and spoke as I thought, "Finally, I am not his victim anymore."

I thought about all of the craziness that had gone on that night. I was thinking about how fluent and graceful Anaghia was as she moved through the room when the flapping wings of a giant nighthawk interrupted my thoughts. The giant bird flew into my room through the opened window. I sat there in admiration of the beautiful, large bird. The hawk landed quietly on the top of my dresser. Its coat was black and shiny like rich, black oil. It stared at me and didn't make any noise. In the reflection from its pitch black eyes I could see myself sitting on the bed. I felt drowsy, as though I was being hypnotized. I blinked and imagined that when I opened my eyes I would see Anaghia. I closed my eyes and heard a fluttering sound. The nighthawk was gone. I walked to the window and looked down into the parking lot. The large, beautiful bird hovered for a while and then landed on the ground. I watched it transform from a nighthawk to a wolf. Then I saw the wolf transform into Anaghia. She stood next to a car with a license plate that read, "CANIS." She looked up at me; and, the next thing I knew, I was staring at her image, one I could see through, in front of me on the balcony outside of my bedroom.

I felt the cool night air encircle and lift me. I moved without effort and glided through the air, around and then down until I, too, was standing next to the car with the license plate that read, "CANIS." I had seen the stars with crystallized clearness as I hovered high above the ground, yet when I touched the ground, I could not remember flying or how I got there. Anaghia was waiting for me. She lowered her head and moved toward me. She greeted me by licking my face, ear and neck. I returned the greeting. She threw her head back and bayed a loud salute and I did the same. We ran fast and free into the front of the apartment complex. Again, those weak creatures were milling around out front. As soon as they saw us they screeched out loud noises and ran into the building. We were not concerned about any of them; we were experiencing the freedom of the world around us. We ran down the street and into the woods. We ran out of the woods and into the streets. We ran for miles and then we walked for miles.

After about an hour, we stopped and sat down. We were back at Shaker Square again. This time, we were in front of a restaurant where several of those weak creatures gathered. The car with the license plate, MYTURN, was parked on the street in front of one of the restaurants. I wondered about the weak creatures that sat behind the clear obstruction. One of them held some familiarity for me. I stopped and stared in hopes I'd be able to remember where I had encountered it before. I listened intently for recognition of sound patterns emitted by the creatures, but nothing was discernable. The creature that I had some familiarity with saw me and quickly ran to get more of its kind. Before long, several of the creatures had gathered behind the clear obstruction. They were pointing at me and screeching out loud noises. Their screeching irritated the calm of the night for me and I became aggravated. I wanted them to stop so I lunged at them but the clear obstruction kept us apart. Anaghia nudged me and we walked down the street. I saw red and blue flashing lights. We ran behind the restaurant and transformed back into ourselves. We walked to the front of the restaurant and went inside. I looked into the face of Jerry as he sat there holding Blascey's hand. He saw me and got scared. He jumped to his feet and ran into the Men's Room. Blascey flashed a look of hatred at me then turned her chair so she could stare at me, face-to-face. I laughed at the potential outcome of her encountering the wolf.

Anaghia touched my shoulder to draw my attention away from Blascey. The look in her eyes and the thought she transferred said, "There is no contest and you know it." She took my hand and said, "I have been waiting for you to come into your spirit for many years."

"I don't quite understand what I'm going through, right now."

"You will."

Jerry walked out of the Men's Room after about five minutes. He couldn't stop staring at Anaghia. She could feel him staring so she turned her seat and stared straight into his eyes. She projected the image of two big wolves tearing him apart on the street into his mind. He wanted to turn away but he couldn't. She had him and would not turn him loose. Jerry was terrified. Anaghia projected that terrifying image into him until he began to shake then she turned her back toward me, signaled the wait staff and ordered a bottle of water. Jerry stood there, stuttering and shaking, unable to speak or move. With an amused smirk on my face, I got up and went into the Ladies' Room. After a few seconds, I heard the bathroom door slam shut behind me. I was standing at the window with my back to the door. I could see the snout in front of my face. This is strange; he's coming out now. I heard the door slam again and then I heard growling. Blascey was standing behind me with that long hatpin in her hand. She held it like a knife. Anaghia had transformed into the wolf and was standing behind her, growling and ready to attack. Blascey dropped the hatpin and tried to open her purse to get her gun. Her purse dropped and Anaghia lunged at her.

Blascey hit the ground with a loud thump. White foam started pouring out of the side of her mouth. Anaghia stood over Blascey but she looked back at me. I, too, had transformed into a wolf. Anaghia back away from Blascey. My paws stretched wide and my long, sharp claws sprung forth. With a long sweeping motion, I struck Blascey, opening her face from the top of her head to her chin. As my claws touched the warm blood that oozed out of her face my understanding of the creatures changed. I understood that Blascey was a human being, and not some weak creature. I saw her as the cold-blooded, calculating, impassionate monster that she was... a heartless female who wanted my life to end...my enemy!

Anaghia knew my understanding had evolved. She looked at me and projected an image of my transformation into a wolf into me. I saw the full beauty of my strength, my body and my ability to survive in her eyes. We transformed back into ourselves. I stood over Blascey and looked down at her. She was not dead but she was afraid to move. She was balled up in a fetal position with her eyes closed tight. I cleared my throat and she opened her eyes. She looked up with one eye opened and the other split opened and oozing with blood.

I leaned down close to her face and said, "Be grateful. I'm letting you live to talk about this...but who will believe you!"

Anaghia and I walked out of the Ladies' Room laughing and talking. We sat down at the table directly behind Jerry and Blascey's table. Jerry got up and walked out the door as though he was about to leave. He walked down the street but in about ten minutes he came back to see about Blascey. Blascey was still in the Ladies' Room, afraid to come out. Jerry said something to the waitress. She pointed to the Ladies' Room. Jerry knocked on the door but Blascey would not answer. Without knowing whether she was okay, Jerry left the restaurant. This time he was angry with Blascey because she was his ride home. He took a cab home.

Anaghia and I sat at the restaurant until it closed. Then we frolicked and ran through the entire city of Cleveland for the rest of the night. At daybreak we returned to the apartment complex. We stood at the car talking about the power and allegiance of the wolf. I still didn't know very much about the powers I had but I was certainly willing to learn more. Anaghia got into her car and drove away. I looked up at my bedroom and saw that the light was on. That could only mean Jerry was there, waiting for me.

Again, a somber, sad feeling came over me. I let out a long sigh and went into the building. I talked to the doorman for a while and then I walked slowly to the elevator. I stood in the elevator without punching any buttons so I could savor the rest of my experience a few minutes longer. Finally, I pressed the button for the twenty-sixth floor. I got to my floor within seconds. I took a deep breath, walked five steps and I was at my door. I closed my eyes as I stuck the key in the door. I unlocked the door and quickly jerked it open. The light was on in the bedroom but the rest of the apartment was dark. Jerry was not there. I put the chain lock on the door to make sure he would not be able to get in without my knowledge. I walked through the dark living room and dining room and I walked into the bedroom without making a sound. I looked in every corner of the room and the closets and I looked under the bed. I didn't trust Jerry and at that point I felt he would try anything to harm me. I smelled cologne, but the scent was becoming weaker and weaker. At the rate it was dissipating I assumed Jerry had been gone for about five minutes. I turned the light off and sat on the edge of my bed. I glanced over at the clock just as the big hand landed on the six in the six-thirty hour.

I woke to the sound of the alarm clock ringing and a loud, rambunctious sounding voice that said, "GIT UP CLEVELAND... It's six fifty-seven and time for you to git up! This is WABQ radio and you're listening to Chucky Charles,

Jr.!" Before the next word came out, the clock was on the floor, broken into several pieces.

"That's the third radio in two weeks, I've got to get to bed earlier," I said in an agitated, soft whisper. "Six-fifty-seven, I didn't even get thirty minutes of sleep."

In the next second I was thinking, well, that's what you get. I could not help wondering if I had just had the most amazing experience of my life or if I had just dreamed the most exhausting but amazing dream of my life.

I heard Jerry in the hallway banging on the door and rattling the chain on the lock. "Take the damn chain off of the door, will you?" he demanded.

By his aggressive behavior, I started to believe I had been dreaming. He didn't seem afraid or intimidated in the least bit. So, what else could it have been? I ignored Jerry and went into the bathroom to shower. I stared into the mirror for a while trying to find traces of the wolf. I saw nothing but I did notice my eyes were almond shaped and medium colored brown. The iris of my eyes had a light yellowish green band in the center of them, unlike the dark, dark brown ring I thought I'd see. I realized at that point I had never looked so closely at myself before. I had the distinct but strange feeling I was looking at someone other than myself. I was delighted with this discovery and I smiled at the thought that the old me was gone. The old me was a victim. This person on the other side of the mirror was courageous, unimpressed or unfazed by the demands of Jerry or anyone else.

I showered and dressed and then we, the person on the inside of me and I, opened the door and left for work.

Jerry was angry when I opened the door. It had taken me at least fifteen minutes to shower and dress. His eyes were squinting and drawn into tight little slits. His look was deceiving, he looked like he was smiling but he was really gritting his teeth and clenching his jaws. As I walked past him he opened his mouth to say something. Without a rational reason, I started laughing and singing,

"Ding dong the witch is dead, the wicked witch, the witch is dead, ding dong the wicked witch is dead."

I laughed and got onto the elevator and let the door shut while he stood there. I was laughing so hard I was crying when I got off of the elevator. The man next door was in the lobby. He thought I was crying from some sort of emotional pain. He rushed to my side to help me. I couldn't stop laughing. I looked at him and laughed even harder. Tears were rolling down my face and I screamed from the pain that was building up in my stomach. I fell forward to a crouching position. I tried to straighten my body but I could not. He realized I was laughing instead of crying and he was embarrassed for trying to help me. He turned and walked away quickly. He stopped at the door and held it open. He had a look of betrayal and hurt on his face.

He said, "I was going to give you a ride to work but you don't want a ride do you?"

I looked at him and even more tears streamed down my face. The laughter was caught somewhere between my stomach and my throat. My mouth was opened but no sound would come out. I rocked back and forth trying to get the word, "No," out but it just would not come. My neighbor realized I was now laughing at him instead of whatever it was that had me bent over in the first place. He became angry and left me sitting there. He walked quickly to his car and slammed the door. I couldn't get his image out of my mind. I could see him standing in the hallway with that platter of gourmet fruits and cheeses and the Grande Année splattering all over his satin smoking jacket as he stood there with his arms stretched out for a hug. The look on his face would be forever engraved in my mind. That moment was meant to be a Kodak moment.

I watched his car pull off and finally I was able to choke out the words, "I don't want a ride," I wanted to stop laughing but I just couldn't.

I could see his large eyes glaring at me in his rear view mirror as he pulled away from the curb. Before I knew it several people were sitting on the lobby furniture laughing with me. They were all laughing and could not stop.

Finally, one girl got her breath and asked, "What are we laughing at?"

"The witch is dead," I blurted out.

She had a very curious look on her face but still she laughed along with the rest of us and together, we walked out of the apartment laughing with tears rolling down our faces.

"The witch is dead!" the girl said.

I shook my head, still laughing and said, "Yes, the wicked witch is dead."

She stopped and said, "Okay, so what's funny about that?"

I looked at her and laughed even harder. "You would have had to have been there," I stuttered out.

CHAPTER TEN

I sat at my desk anxiously awaiting the arrival a professor I worked for. Her name was Dr. Javan. She was a very liberated, free-spirited, individual who was open to experience all of the little nuances life has to offer. She seemed to have a different take on life than anyone I'd ever met before. I wanted her opinion of what I had experienced or dreamed, or whatever it was. She normally got to work at about ten o'clock AM. At ten o'clock and one second I was in front of her office door. She wasn't there. I was busting at the seams. I needed to talk to her about what had happened. I could see Thomas, a professor with whom my relationship was becoming more problematic on a daily basis, peering at me from his office. I saw him shuffle his papers a few times and then get up and walk to the door. He was the one professor I wanted to avoid at all costs. We used to be what I assumed were friends, or at the very least, we were friendly toward each other. For some reason, in a period of a month or two, his attitude toward me changed. He began to resent the fact I used my office for my personal business, which was to solicit and interview models. And, he hated the idea I was able to hold my fashion shows in the university auditorium. Why? I'll never know because God in Heaven knew none of those things I did had anything to do with him, nor did it interfere with the work I did for him. I assumed he just didn't like my personality and he was willing to use anything he could to justify his personal dislike for me. Aside from disliking my personality, at times, he made me feel like he hated me because I had questions about some of his ideas and directives. It was as though I challenged his authority or didn't have a right to think in his presence.

I was due for a raise and I was expecting a great one because my work ethics and work had always been outstanding. I had gone way beyond the call of duty taking on projects and assisting everyone in the department. Thomas saw his chance to exact a punishment on me, or get back at me, or whatever it was he felt he needed to do to bring me into submission to him. He gave me an 'AVERAGE' performance rating because I had made a few typing errors in a book he was writing.   In those days books were not typed on a computer where you could backspace and type over an error. They were typed on manual typewriters using bond paper and carbon paper for the copies. Correcting an error was done with a razor blade and a white stick. His first draft had about two thousand pages to be typed. On each page there were about three hundred words and, in all, I made about sixty errors in the entire book. That was an outstanding ratio by all standards and he gave me an AVERAGE rating.   Well, I was fit to be tied. I was not about to stand for that insult. 'Average,' ... the idea and the word went through me like a razor cutting paper. I was emotionally shredded by that word! I had to turn away from him to make sure my mouth was not hanging open with surprise.   When he formed his mouth to state what type of performance rating I was getting, I was just sure he was about to say, excellent! I hit the ceiling when the word 'average' dripped out. I could barely contain myself. I looked at him with daggers that could have sliced him in half. I had to count to ten before I could respond to him.   After counting to ten I took a deep breath and exhaled slowly.   Finally, I regained my composure and asked him a few questions. I was cordial and cool when questioning him about his rating system but I was still burning up inside.

Thomas refused to answer my questions so I took the matter up with our department head, Dr. Kotterstanz, and the Dean of the Business College, Dr. Charles. In our meeting Thomas told them I was arrogant and cocky. Both Dr. Kotterstanz and Dr. Charles were familiar with my work and me. I had pinch hit for their assistants in the past. On many occasions, they both requested my help for personal projects they had going on. In addition, I worked with both of them on the Master's Program Committee and ended up administering the program at their request. Dr. Kotterstanz asked Thomas how 'cocky and arrogant' translated into 'average' on my performance review. Thomas had a look of shock and disdain on his face. It was as though they, too, had betrayed him and now they were as cocky and arrogant as I had been. At any rate, he couldn't answer the question to any of our satisfaction. When he was asked what work

I had done at an average level he told them I had a lot of models coming into my office. Again, he didn't answer the question. They asked him if I got my work done when he needed it.

He said, "Yes, but, she's arrogant when she gives it to me."

Dr. Charles seemed to be particularly and extremely interested in how I showed my arrogance. He had expressed to me on several occasions I was too humble.

Thomas made the mistake of saying, "She leaves my work in her Out Box and when I walk into her room I expect her to hand it to me." He went on to say, "She walks with her head held so high she looks like she's looking down on everyone else."

"Anything else?" Dr. Charles asked.

"Yes, as a matter of fact there is," he answered smugly.

Dr. Kotterstanz sat straight in his chair. He pinched his glasses and slid them to the tip of his nose, as he did when he was irritated. He looked at Thomas squarely in his eyes and said, "Well, are we going to have to guess here, or are you going to tell us what else she did to make you think she was acting arrogantly?"

Thomas scooted to the edge of his chair as though he had the bullet that blew away the bandit. He looked over at me like I was the bandit he was about to blow away. Then he said, "As I reviewed her performance with her, she objected to my comments. And, when I gave her my final assessment...which was her performance was average, she said, "I don't do average. You'll have to show me how, where and when my work was average. Clearly she made some typing mistakes in my manuscript. Sixty to be exact."

When he said that, in my mind's eye, I could see a bullet slowly exiting the chamber of the gun, making a sharp U-turn and burrowing its way into his forehead. I could almost hear the cracking sound of a bullet shattering his bones.

If anyone had been looking at me at the moment, they would have had to wonder what on earth I was looking at because I stared at Thomas' forehead with gleeful anticipation of the bullet's final impact. Both, Dr. Charles and Dr. Kotterstanz, were published and had had several manuscripts typed for them. They were accustomed to having hundreds of errors in their first drafts. Dr. Charles' assistant was out sick for about two months and I sat in for her. It was during that time I worked with him on one of his manuscripts. He was elated with my work. He couldn't believe how quickly I had completed his drafts and he was amazed by the accuracy. On another occasion, Dr. Kotterstanz's assistant was overwhelmed with work so I offered to help her. Instead of giving me a few small jobs, she gave me his manuscript to type. Normally, it took the two of them a month of working through the night to get that job done. Dr. Kotterstanz liked to proof as you completed the pages. He didn't give you section-by-section like the rest of the professors. He gave you the entire, completed, handwritten manuscript to be typed. In two weeks I had the entire manuscript completed, copied, collated and ready for the editors to review. He could not believe it. After that he changed my schedule to accommodate me typing his next manuscripts. He took me to dinner and we talked about a million and one things. I think we both found each other to be very interesting. He told me my work was amazing. He didn't think it was possible to have that kind of accuracy in a first draft. He was grateful because I was able to save him a great deal of time. He did a few re-writes but those didn't take much time to correct at all. All in all, I'd say we were able to get his book to his editor way ahead of schedule. Dr. Kotterstanz and Dr. Charles knew it was unreasonable for Thomas to expect me to type a perfect first draft. So, Thomas had picked the wrong subject to bring to them as a weakness of mine.

Dr. Charles was extremely irritated with Thomas by this time. He took his glasses off and sat them on the table. He looked at Dr. Kotterstanz with disbelief. Dr. Kotterstanz snatched the performance appraisal off of the table and tore it up. Dr. Charles systematically broke Thomas' defense down to a zero rejection rate. He read off how well I had done and told Thomas he agreed with me, I didn't do average! I thanked them for being fair and walked out of the room. As I pulled the door to close it, I heard Dr. Kotterstanz tell Thomas he was arrogant. He went on to say much more but I had already pulled the door closed and could not hear the rest of what he had to say.

I could hear Thomas shout, "But she used our auditorium for her own personal use."

I couldn't hear Dr. Kotterstanz but I was sure he told him we had negotiated the use of the University and the auditorium as a part of my employment and there was nothing that Thomas could do about it. I wanted to stand outside and listen a bit longer but I was anxious to see Dr. Javan so I left.

When Thomas walked out of Dr. Charles' office he saw me waiting in front of Dr. Javan's door. He was angry. He walked up to me in a very threatening manner. He got so close to me it looked like he was going to kiss me. Several students passed us in the hallway but they could not hear what he said.

He clenched his jaws and gritted his teeth as he spoke, "You tried to make me look stupid in there!"

I started to answer him but he put his hand up and gestured for me not to speak. I stood there and let him get everything he wanted to say, out. My anger was building in me in a way it never had before. I could hear my heart beat in my ears, the blood in my veins felt so hot that I felt like I was being burned from the inside out. I felt strength surge throughout my body just like I did when the wolf appeared to me the night before. At that point, I knew I had the upper hand, I could subdue him and control the outcome of our encounter and that was exactly what I intended to do. No more Miss Nice Guy! This new feeling was invigorating. It was great, especially after feeling so helpless for such a long time.

I saw Thomas in a totally new way that day and I came to know myself for the first time as a whole, strong woman who could take care of herself. I saw him as weak and confused and I was strong and in control. I knew he didn't know what to do and his only way of solving what he perceived as a problem, was to lash out at it. Well, I was not his problem and I wasn't about to allow him to lash out at me! He was so busy trying to bully me he didn't notice the change in me.

He poked his finger into my shoulder and said, "I will have your job before the end of the year. I don't like you. You are arrogant and insubordinate."

The strength in my hands and arms was unyielding. I was shaking trying to keep them at my side. I felt like I could lift the building without breaking a sweat. I looked at my arms and hands and I saw red and blue veins running up and down them like railroad tracks. They were still skinny and small but they were galvanized with strength. I looked back up at Thomas and I realized how much damage I could do to him if I wanted to. Instead, I waited patiently for him to finish. I could feel my teeth flashing as my lips pulled back to a tight grimace. I looked at him and saw a shallow image of a man trying to fake a strong appearance. I could see the confusion in his eyes. I watched him back away, little by little, until he was about a foot away from me. Still, caught up in his anger and confusion, he failed to notice the change in me.

After he delivered what he thought was the threat of a lifetime, he tried to turn to walk away from me. I grabbed the sharply pressed edges of his shirt's shoulder panels and pushed him against the wall. His eyes widened like round half dollars and a tear popped into his left eye as his head hit the hard concrete wall.

I said in a soft whisper, "You touch me again, Thomas, and not only will I have you up on charges but I will personally tear you into pieces." I could hear a deep dog-like growl come from inside of me as I spoke.

His legs were shaking like leaves and his arms were wiggling like worms. I felt no sympathy for him at all. I didn't like him and I wanted him to know it.

I smiled slightly as I spoke, "I will be perfectly clear with you on this point and I want you to understand me without a doubt. I don't care if you like me or not. I don't want your friendship and I don't like working for you. You are a self-serving, egotistical airhead who can't tell good work from good behavior. Whatever you think about me doesn't matter to me in the least bit."

I turned his body away from the wall and pushed him away from me. I turned to walk away from him but I stopped and stepped as close to him as he had to me. I penetrated him with my eyes as I growled out the words, "Do not make the mistake of thinking I will not hurt you. I will tear you to shreds if you ever touch me or try to pull another stunt like this against me. Do you understand me, clearly?" Another deep growl came from inside of me. I could see fear and intimidation in his eyes as he shook his head up and down in agreement. At that point I don't think he would have refused anything I asked.

Not only could I see the fear in his eyes, I could feel his fear in his heart, I could smell it. It radiated off of his body like waves of a cold, icy, relentless wind. What Thomas didn't realize was that everyone we worked with basically disliked him and everyone, basically, liked me. Thomas was one of those people whose title defined him. He was not a person, he was a professor and he thought his word weighed more heavily than mine with the college administration because I was just an administrative assistant.

Dr. Javan stood about a foot behind me. I didn't know she was there. Thomas saw her and he shouted, "You saw her push me against the wall, didn't you?"

"I saw and heard everything!" She looked angry. She turned to Thomas and continued, "I saw you poke her and threaten her first! Thomas, what were you thinking?" Then she turned to me and said, "And you, I can't believe your reaction. Don't you think you overreacted?" She went on to say, "I heard both of you threaten each other. So, I'd say you guys are even. Wouldn't you?"

Thomas shook his head, "Yes," then he paused and said, "How could you hear what I said. I was whispering."

She exploded with, "It doesn't matter, Thomas, I heard you threaten her. What the hell were you thinking?"

I wanted to smile but I held it in. I looked at both of them and said, "I don't want this to go any further. I think Dr. Charles can resolve this problem."

Thomas' eyes pleaded with me not to go to Dr. Charles again. Our meeting of earlier that day was already the third time one of the administrative staff had taken him before the Dean, not to mention the number of students who had filed complaints against him. My complaint may just have been the magical ingredient that it would take to put a mark on his record; or, the one that would have at least put an imprint of Dr. Charles' boot on his butt.

Dr. Javan put her bag in her office and we went to my office to talk. In private, Dr. Javan told me I was right but I had responded badly to his intimidation tactics.

She also said, "Good for you, though. That guy can be such a pill. It's about time somebody shot back at him."

I didn't want to waste anymore time talking about Thomas. I said, "He's not important. I've got to get your advice on something. I mean, something is happening to me and I don't know what to think about it."

I could tell by the expression on her face her curiosity was piqued. She let out a long, questioning sigh and then said, "Okay, but I've got to say this…you surprised me today. I had come to know you as a very mild mannered person who would not stand up for yourself in a situation like that, "she sighed again and said, "Your mannerism and your actions were not congruent. Your mannerisms are those of a meek person who would avoid conflict at all cost but you roared like a lion a few minutes ago and I was glad to see it!"

I smiled and said, "More like growled like a wolf."

Her eyes widened even more with curiosity. She said, "You know, I thought I heard some sort of growl but I thought…No, couldn't have been and I dismissed it. So is that what you want to talk about? This growl?"

Thomas was milling around outside of my door for a while before the pressure got to him and he burst into my office in a rage. Both, Dr. Javan and I ignored him. We went on talking as if he was not in the room. I wanted to tell her all about my experience but she had to leave for a class. She had classes until one thirty that afternoon. We decided to have a late lunch so we could talk without interruption. I walked her back to her office. When I got back to mine, there was a note on my desk from Thomas marked 'PERSONAL AND CONFIDENTIAL.' I left the note on my desk untouched.

CHAPTER ELEVEN

Dr. Javan and I had lunch at Russo's, a quaint little Italian restaurant, around the corner from the university. It was one of the campus hotspots. Most of the students frequented it every night for the jazz and rock sessions. Every Thursday night they had open mic for all of the local spoken word artists and singers. It was a great place to go, either alone or with friends. Whenever you'd get there, you'd see somebody you knew and if you didn't, everybody in the place was introducing him or herself to you and offering to buy you drinks. I had never seen it so empty before. There were only a few people in the restaurant because of the lateness of the day. I told her what happened and I didn't know if I was awake or asleep. She seemed to be enchanted. She was bewitched by what I told her and focused all of her attention on the actions of the wolf. To her, my being awake or asleep was incidental. It had no real value. She asked a number of questions about the way I felt right before and after the wolf appeared. I really couldn't give her any answers because I was so focused on what had happened while I was inside of the wolf I hadn't thought about anything else. I was saddened at the thought that the way I felt was of no consequence to anyone, not even to me. I had become accustomed to putting everyone else's thoughts and needs before my own. Before the wolf my feelings just didn't matter and didn't really register, like I said, not even with me. And, after he left all I did was pine for him to come back because being a part of him made me come alive and matter. She pushed me to answer her question but I couldn't. The only thing I knew was I didn't feel strange or anything else before he appeared. The wolf's snout was suddenly in front of me and I was inside of him, looking out at the world and feeling his confidence and strength and that was it! He was there and I was inside of him or I was he.

Dr. Javan believed the Indian folklore about Native American Indians shape-shifting into wolves. She asked question after question about my heritage. I remembered looking at a picture of an old Indian woman on a farm in my mother's collection of pictures. The picture looked sort of cartoonish to me. It looked like it was hand-drawn and painted with watercolors. It turned out to be a picture of my great, great, great grandmother.

"That's it," she said with a big smile on her face. In her mind she had solved the mystery. She knew many African slaves had married Native American Indians in many parts of the south. So, in her mind, that was the only answer for my experience.

"What?" I asked.

She told me wolves were sacred animals to many Native American Indian tribes and the spirit of the wolf protected them. She surmised I was in some kind of danger and the wolf was there to protect me. She insisted I find out about my family heritage and I find someone in the family who may have heard some of the folklore about our family and wolves. I really didn't want to ask anyone in the family about wolves because I knew they would think I was just crazy, but this was important, regardless of what they'd think about me. I kept thinking, what if he wasn't real...what if I made him up because my life was such a bore I needed a diversion. I felt torn in my heart. I wanted to believe the wolf had been there with me and had protected me but at the same time, I didn't want the belief in the wolf to interfere with my religious beliefs. After all, what would that say about my belief in God? Why would I need the protection of a wolf if my faith were in God? She posed that and several more questions back to me.

"What does that say about your belief in God? Do you still believe in Him? Is He powerful enough to send you a physical representation of strength when you need one? Or, do you think God would just leave you to be raped, beaten savagely and possibly killed by two men who had no good in mind when they saw you? Do you believe God would allow some woman and your husband to harm you when all you have done is to be good to him and accommodate him when you didn't even want to? Is that the kind of God you serve? What do you think about your faith in God? Why does this manifestation have to interfere with your faith?

My only answer was, "Yes, without a doubt I do believe in God. And, I do believe He can send me something or someone and even some animal to help me in my time of need."

In that brief moment, my issue with my faith was resolved. I believed without a doubt that God has angels watching over and giving aide to us when we need it. Who was to say the wolf was not my angel? I had to laugh as I thought about the image of angels I'd had for most of my life and only I would end up with my angel being a big ferocious wolf. I didn't see any wings on him but I was willing to acknowledge that he was an angel sent by God to help me.

After a few minutes of going over the oddity of my angel, I convinced myself my faith was intact. I smiled again to myself and said softly, "Whatever it takes…huh God? Whatever it takes!"

In those few minutes I had almost forgotten Dr. Javan was even in the room. When she spoke, she startled me. What she said shocked me even more. In a very calm and matter-of-fact manner she told me she was a witch and she was a part of a group of witches that studied a religion called Wiccan. Normally, I would have been afraid to even talk to her because of the evil connotations I associated with the word 'witch,' but she was different. The only image I had of witches in those days was what I had seen on television. I envisioned witches to be long, skinny women dressed in black, sitting around human-sized, pot-bellied caldrons, dropping herbs, cattails, eye of lizard and children into pots of boiling water. I also had a vision of long-nosed women with big warts on their noses flying through the air on crooked broomsticks in the black of the night casting sinister shadows across the moon. Strangely enough, I was not fearful of her, but I was curious. She wasn't evil or mean. She explained the type of witch she was and told me she did do spells but they were spells that did good for people and protected her from evil. I left her feeling there must be some good witches because she was such a nice person. I also felt challenged. I needed to find out more about my family's history.

My mother, her brother and sister were deceased at the time but she did have a younger sister, Aunt Aniee, who was still living. She was very ill, though. Questioning her about such a thing was out of the question. Aunt

Aniee took her ways after my Grandma Mindy. They both were kind of hard to predict, nice one day and hateful as sin the next. With failing health, I was not about to bother her with my wolf situation. I exhausted her in any way I would suffer the wrath of Aunt Aniee's two sons. Both of them had the personality of wild dogs that had just been fed gun powder. I'd just have to find another source for information. Most of the time Aunt Aniee was very warm and nice to me but still I stayed out of her way. As a small child, I had had one bad experience with her that I just didn't want to have repeated so I stayed away from her most of my life. If I had asked her a question about our family turning into wolves she would not have just called me crazy but she would have convinced the rest of the family I was crazy.

I stopped at a pay phone and called my brother, Bill, to ask if he knew anything about our family and any wolves. I could tell by the way he answered my question and how deliberately he pronounced his words he thought something was wrong with me. I think he thought I was losing my mind. I also called my Aunt Evelyn, who was a pretty good family historian, to ask her, but she didn't know anything about any wolves. Aunt Evelyn married my mother's brother when she was thirteen years old and, at the time, she was well into her seventies. She knew about my great, great, great grandmother and several other Indian and African slave ancestors in my family. She told me some great stories but nothing that related to wolves. She told me one of my great, great, great, great uncles used to roam the woods with bears and others in the family believed he shape-shifted into a bear. Hearing that made me believe shape shifting was a possibility for the people in my family and I wasn't falling off the deep end of the earth with this notion of being a wolf. By the time the thought had completed in my mind, Aunt Evelyn was calling him crazy and delusional. I dismissed her comments and held on to the belief that what had happened to me the other night was a real possibility. I was enthralled at the thought I could actually have been that strong, fierce animal whose presence created fear and trembling among all whom had seen it.

When I got back to my office the note Thomas had written was sitting on my seat. It read, I am willing to drop this whole thing if you are. And, by the way, none of this would have ever happened if you had paid a little more attention to me. You seem to laugh and joke with everyone but me. Why don't you like me? I like you more than you know. This is your fault!!!!!! He had taken it out of the envelope. It lay open on the seat of my chair. The note wasn't signed but it was on his stationery and it was definitely his handwriting.

I didn't want to think he had been treating me so poorly just because he wanted to become intimate with me. Knowing Thomas, I could have been misreading his intentions from the note but I would never find out because everything he did seemed to have some sort of covert mission behind it. In actuality, everything he did was a reaction that stemmed from his paranoia. Thomas read betrayal in every action anyone has ever done. In his mind, everyone was plotting against him. How he ever got as far as he did in life was a mystery to everyone around him and to me. I assumed he had done so much dirt to so many people he projected his underhandedness onto everyone else and he expected everyone to act and react like he did. I did realize one very important thing after reading that note, and that was, I was dealing with a man on the edge! I could have brought harassment charges against him but it wouldn't have been worth the trouble.

As I read the note I felt someone looking at me. I looked up but no one was there. I got up to close my door and a flurry of papers scattered and blew across the front of it. Thomas had been watching me read his note and was hiding outside. He didn't try to pick up his papers; instead, he ran to his office and slammed his door. I picked up the papers and took them to him. I wanted to ask him if he felt silly for running away but at the same time, I didn't want to prolong our conversation any longer than necessary. He could not look at me. His eyes glazed past me as they sprinted around the room. Again, I wondered how such a shallow, silly man could be someone who had made it through college and had become a professor. I knew his wife had money and he used the influence that went along with her money for practically everything. But, I thought he met and married her after he had become a professor. I stood there without saying anything for a few minutes. His face was contorting as he sat in silence. He looked like he was in real pain and I wanted to feel sorry for him but I just could not. His eyes were pleading with me and he had a sad, clown-like look on his face. I was unaffected but I didn't show it. I allowed my eyes to close somewhat to appear like there was sympathy in them. In actuality, I wanted to throw his papers at him and leave but I figured if I conceded and extended my hand in friendship, maybe this cold war between us could be over. I just could not go through another extended period of time fighting with him and trying to avoid him. And, with my newfound courage and strength hiding from him was the last thing I was going to do. Fighting with me should have been the last thing he should have wanted to do.

At any rate, I was ready to be done with all of the battling back and forth and just let the whole thing go. Thomas was one of those manipulative people who read other people well and then used their emotions against them. He must have read the fight fatigue in my face.

"You read my note?"

I shook my head and said, "Yes."

"So, can we call a truce?"

I answered without hesitation, "Certainly."

"So, why don't we have dinner to draft the terms of the truce?"

I wanted it to be over but I didn't want to have dinner with him. He was the last person with whom I wanted to spend any of my free time. I had been told my feelings show on my face and I was sure if Thomas could read faces like I thought he could then he knew mine was saying, "Are you out of your mind, man?" I could see he was up to his old trick of trying to manipulate the situation and me.

I said with a scowl in my voice, "Dinner?"

"Yes, dinner." he retorted angrily.

At that point I was ready to do whatever battle necessary to get him off of my back. I felt assured he had lost his mind. Still, I didn't want a confrontation so I asked if we could just draft the terms right then and there.

He shouted, "No. I said I want to have dinner!"

I shook my head in disbelief. I became angrier and angrier. I felt the blood flush throughout my face and I could hear my heart pounding in my ears.

"You have absolutely no common sense, do you Thomas? I mean you must have lost your damn mind. Why on earth would I want to spend my time sitting down to dinner with you? You just can't quit when you are ahead can you? You have to put your damn foot into the pot, too. Don't you!"

His face turned red with embarrassment and anger. He had shown himself to be incapable of handling this conflict in a mature manner in the past and I was ready for whatever he was about to bring to the table.

"Oh...you will have dinner with Dr. Kotterstanz and Dr. C and lunch with Dr. Javan but you won't have dinner with me!" He began to pout like a child. He poked his bottom lip out and kicked the desk. He grabbed the papers in his In-Box and crumpled them up and threw them across the room.

I didn't say a word I just walked away.

He screamed, "If you want to keep your job you had better reconsider my offer!" Then he hollered, "Why don't you like me? I'll have you fired. Dr. C is not the last word here. I'll have you fired."

Without stopping I spoke softly as I walked away, "Don't you dare threaten me Thomas. If you think I frightened you in the hallway earlier, you haven't seen anything yet! I am afraid I will hurt you if you don't stop this harassment."

By the time I reached my office and sat in my chair he was standing at my door.

"Did you just say that you were afraid that you would hurt me?" he asked.

I looked directly into his eyes and said, softly, "Yes."

In his arrogance he blurted out, "Hurt me. You can't hurt me. I'm a professor and you are a clerk!"

Surprisingly, I was not angry. I was amused at his arrogance. I smiled and said in a very calm voice, "That's right Thomas, you are a professor. Now, go back into your office like a nice little professor before something bad happens to you, you know you are treading on dangerous ground, right?"

He was turning to walk away from me but I wanted him to stay a moment longer to hear my last thoughts on the matter. I focused on him not being able to move away from the door. I looked at him and it looked like he was trying to pull his hand away from the door's frame but he could not. He also looked like he wanted to turn his body so he could walk away but he could not move.

I thought, but didn't say the words, if you threaten my job again…well, let's just say you won't be able to perform yours! As the thought completed in my mind, he fell to the ground. I walked over to the door, looked at him as he lay on the floor unable to move his hand from the doorframe. Now get out of my doorway. At that same moment, he yanked his hand away from the door and scooted into the hall.

In the next second I slammed the door so hard the glass broke. Thomas was getting up off the floor looking in my office as if he could not believe what had just happened. I did not know whether he heard my thoughts or not, but I felt not being able to pull his hand away from the door had something to do with them. Someone saw the glass fragments on the floor and called the janitor before I had a chance to report it. I looked up from my desk with angry eyes and watched the nimble, quick-witted janitor scurry around cleaning up the broken glass.

"There are no fingers on the floor on the other side of that door, are there?" he laughed.

I tried to muster a pleasant smile and tone but I growled out the words, "Lucky for him," through clenched teeth.

CHAPTER TWELVE

I organized my work and completed it as quickly as possible that day. I did not have any work to do on the Master's program so I finished the work for the university in about ten minutes. The rest of the day I interviewed models, created new routines, and wrote a few skits. Thomas and his childishness did not enter my mind at all. I focused on the wolf when I wasn't thinking about new routines and the models. I truly could not tell which part of my experience was a dream or which part was real. I tried to find bits of evidence to convince myself I was awake but I could never really pinpoint anything specific. I, briefly, thought about Jerry and the thought of him depressed me. Was he trying to have me killed? How could he hate me so much? I, clearly, saw hatred in his eyes. How long had he harbored those feelings?

Three rapid taps and the door opening interrupted my thoughts. Dr. Javan was standing in the doorway panting as though she had been running. Out of breath, and in a haggard voice she said, "I saw the janitor cleaning in front of your door a little earlier, what happened? You splatter Thomas all over the floor."

I was happy to see her. I was so excited I felt like a child who had been away from its parent for the entire day. I laughed and said, "No, but I don't think he'll be messing with me anymore."

"I remember the first day we met," she said as she exhaled a long, deep breath. She stopped and bent over to catch her breath and then she walked over and sat on the edge of my desk. Still grasping for air, she said, "I remember the day we met. I saw you coming toward me and I was backed up into my office."

"What do you mean you were backed up?"

"Your energy and the protective forces around you were strong and impenetrable. By the time, you reached my office I was in my chair and I could not get up to greet you. My energy was not gone but it was as if something held it down and would not allow it to surface. It was like an invisible hand held me down in that chair!"

I also remembered thinking she looked as though something was pushing her down and would not release her.

She went on to say, "See, before I meet anyone new…or whenever a new person will be a part of my life, and of course, you were going to be a big part of my life since we would be working together, I tap into the universal power of darkness and light and it allows me to direct the interactions that are to take place with that person. The universe responds to me in kind, you know." Still gasping for air she continued, "I am required to perform certain deeds and my energy is transformed and directed around me as a sort of protective shield. Sounds mysterious, I know. Anyway, I had spells I cast for special purposes but I was prohibited from casting a spell on you. As a matter of fact, on that day, I woke up feeling as though I was under some kind of attack but I wasn't under attack, I just didn't have any powers. So, I took special precautions to protect myself from evil forces but nothing worked. You immobilized me."

I didn't know what to think. "You mean I was an evil force?" I asked softly.

"No, no you weren't. You were a force. Not evil and not good but a powerful force that would prove itself later...and I guess now is later," she said with a huge smile on her face.

The doorknob rattled and the door flung open. Thomas blocked the doorway; he was breathing hard and grumbling something, incomprehensible, under his breath. Then he blurted out, "Why are you prolonging this? You went to the Dean! I told you I wanted it to be over. You tell me why the hell Dr. Charles is calling to see me now?"

I shook my head in disbelief and rolled my eyes from aggravation. I did not respond to him because I did not have anything to do with Dr. Charles calling him. I waved him off with my hand.

He shouted, "Don't you wave me off! Don't you dare wave me off! Who do you think you are?"

Dr. Javan looked at her watch and said excitedly, "We'll finish this later. It's important." Then she rushed out of the room in the same flustered, hurried way she had entered.

Thomas was still angry but he did calm down quite a bit. He composed himself and asked, "Did you go to Dr. Charles on me after we agreed that it was over?"

I was irritated with him and tired of him. I let out a long sigh to let him know I was tired and bored with his behavior. I looked at him with my eyes half closed and yawned, I said, "No, no, I didn't call Dr. Charles. Maybe it was one of the other underlings you offend so often!"

He had a strange look on his face. He dropped his head and said in an almost child-like voice, "You've changed. I can't put my finger on it but I like it even less."

I sat there stoic and unimpressed with his newfound discovery and feelings for me.

"Is there something you want from me, Thomas?"

He stood up slowly, his head hung down and his voice was shaky, "Yes, yes there is something I want."

I was annoyed with him and I wanted him out of my office. "Tell me what you want to happen here." I said angrily.

He looked at me with an orphaned looked in his eyes, as if he had no one to turn to and wanted me to take him in, "I want us to be okay."

"Okay? What does okay mean, Thomas?"

He walked over to the door and snatched the doorknob. In a flash, he had changed from a sad, boy-like child to angry old heathen with revenge in his heart and he was ready to leave. This time he had a rage in his voice I had not detected before.

"You misunderstand me. You are making fun of me. I knew you were going to be a problem."

That is when I considered the idea that Thomas was probably schizophrenic. And, it was then I realized how fragile he was so I decided I would have to be the one to submit if our feuding was ever going to end.

I took his hand and led him back to the seat at my desk. "Thomas, we don't have to get along so badly. I don't dislike you, at all. I dislike the way you treat everyone here who is not a tenured professor or a dean and me. Why do you make such a difference in the way you treat people?"

He looked at me like I was some homeless person who had just climbed out of a garbage bin with a chicken bone hanging out of my mouth begging for pennies to buy a swig of rotgut. Disdain was all over his face. He may as well have said, what are you doing talking to someone like me, you peon? How dare you look at me you uncultured heathen! And, how dare you question my treatment of the lesser of this earth...you poor person, you!   Instead, he looked past me at the door and said, "I don't make a difference in the way I treat you guys."

I did not have the patience for whatever game he was playing. I walked back over to the door and stood there. This time, I waited for him to leave.

He started to get out of the seat when he asked, "Do you really think I'm an elitist?"

My answer came before I realized my mouth had opened, "Yes, don't you?" I looked at the clock on the wall. His class would be starting in fifteen minutes and my two forty-five appointment was due in ten minutes. "Thomas, why don't we talk about this after your class? You're giving an exam today aren't you?"

He looked at his watch and said, "I want to talk, now. I think we're making headway."

I stood there wondering what he had just experienced and where I was when the headway was being made, but I decided not to question him. I guessed he felt that way because this was the first time we hadn't avoided each other in a long time.

"I'll give Marlene the exams and she can get them started. That way we can talk as long as we need to."

I didn't trust him and certainly not his desire to talk. I knew he had an ulterior motive. He was not being nice to me because he wanted us to get along. This had something to do with Dr. Charles I knew I would have to wait him out...let him show his hand first. I could see he wanted to play a game of cat and mouse. What he did not see was I was about to play the wolf.

I walked quickly to my desk to pick up the phone. As soon as I reached for it, it rang.

"Yes, that will be fine. Why don't I call you in a week?"

"Expecting a call at two thirty-five, huh?" Thomas whispered.

"Yes, two thirty-five exactly."

I took my weekly reminder out of my purse and sat it on my desk so I would remember to pencil in the new appointment. He slid out of the chair and walked backwards to the door, watching me as he moved away.

When he reached the door I said, "I thought you wanted to talk now."

"I'll just give you something to think about," he said as he bumped into the doorframe. "I really do like you. I like you quite a lot. I want to get to know you a lot better than I know you right now."

"I don't like to play guessing games, Thomas. That sounds like it could be an invitation to get to know me better as a co-worker and it also sounds like you want to get to know me on an intimate basis. Which is it?"

His face turned red and he said in a sheepish voice, "It is both but we are not co-workers, you are my subordinate. That's what it is, though, it is both." He turned and ran down the hall.

"What the hell," I said in a low and astonished voice, "What the hell, now?"

CHAPTER THIRTEEN

I was about to get up but I reached for the phone instead. As my hand touched the cradle, it rang.

"The phone didn't even ring. Expecting a call from someone?" The voice said on the other end.

"How can I help you?"

"This is your husband what the hell do you mean, how can you help me?"

"How can I help you?" I repeated.

The phone got quiet. After about thirty seconds he said, "We need to talk, don't you think?"

"Yes, go ahead, what is it you want to say?"

While Jerry talked, I began writing in my calendar and typing a routine.

"Are you listening to me?" he quipped.

"You haven't said anything." I replied in a calm and uninterested tone.

Normally, I would have been emotionally torn. I knew our marriage had ended a number of years ago but we were about to move away from each other. It was about to end for good and it didn't matter in the least bit to me. It was no more emotional than taking off an old pair of shoes and throwing them away.

"You act like you hate me," he said in a surprised voice.

"No, hate is too strong a sentiment. I don't hate you; I have no feelings for you at all."

"Well," he demanded, "We'll see about that when you don't have me anymore. You know how many women are just waiting to get their hands on me."

"Better them than me." I laughed.

I had the warmest feeling as I thought about pieces of him being torn up and thrown around the room.

I asked again, "How may I help you, Jerry?"

He became enraged and his words became garbled. He blurted out, "What the hell is in you? You are acting like you are somebody else. Like I did something so wrong that other men haven't done. I told you, I didn't have anything to do with Blascey. She's just like a groupie. She just wants to be seen with somebody important."

"Somebody important," I laughed.

I had just heard the most ridiculous statement I'd ever heard in my life. Over the past couple of years I had the distinct impression Jerry was becoming more and more caught up in an image he had created of himself. I thought but could never prove Jerry thought of himself as a celebrity. I laughed out loud at how absurd his words were. What in the world would make him think he would have groupies of all things? In a split second, I was seeing Jerry running his hand along the edge of his pants pocket. The hatpin was in his pocket and the cap had been jarred loose.

"Hey," I said, "You better be careful or you're gonna stick yourself with that hatpin."

The phone went silent first and then the cradle hit the edge of the table. I could hear Jerry fumbling around trying to pick it up. The next thing I heard was dial tone. He had hung up on me.

I couldn't help wonder where and when things went wrong between Jerry and me. I didn't hate him but I certainly didn't love him. In fact, the more I thought about it, the more I realized I never did love him. I kept expecting to fall in love with him but it just never happened. I thought about the night I met him. It was the night of my ten-year class reunion. I was one of the organizers and he was there. He wasn't an alumni and he wasn't there with anyone from Kennedy. He went to John Hay, Kennedy's archrival.   A few months earlier, I had narrowly escaped from a horrible relationship with a man I called Tic. Tic was short for lunatic. It had been almost three months and this was my first night out to a public affair, without a date, since getting away from Tic. I was just getting accustomed to being alone and I was enjoying it. I really just wanted to get the announcements and preliminary business out of the way, reacquaint myself with old school chums, dance to my favorite records and go home.   When I got there I saw Jack, a good friend of mine.   Since my brother was out of town, Jack had become my surrogate big brother.   He became very protective of me after I got away from Tic.   He was Aleena's boyfriend. I introduced them and they hit it off righteously. They had so much in common it was unreal. They even looked a little alike. Jack had a way of showing up at events I was involved with ever since I got away from Tic. I think Aleena was sending him out to watch over me whenever she knew I'd be alone. He motioned for me to sit with him.

He smiled as he spoke, "I knew you'd be alone, so I decided to keep you company, otherwise, I wouldn't have come tonight."

I saw Jerry sitting across the room and I tried, very hard, not to look at him but my eyes were glued on him when I answered Jack, "Thanks, Jack. What would I do without a good friend like you?"

As soon as I put my coat on the seat Jack asked me to dance. Jerry stared at me the entire time. I was flattered. He was tall and handsome and he flashed the most perfect smile I had ever seen. I learned later he spent hours in the mirror practicing that smile. I tried to keep my back to Jerry so I wouldn't stare at him. The next thing I knew he was tapping Jack on the shoulder asking to cut in on our dance. Both, Jack and I were surprised. We had never seen or known anyone to cut in on a dance before. I had seen people cut in on dances on television, but that was television.

"This ain't Parma, partner! You don't cut in on a man's dance in Cleveland, Ohio."

Jerry ignored Jack and tapped him on the shoulder again.

Jack said, "What, what...you got a problem? Man, what did I just say to you? What is it … you don't understand English. What is the problem?"

Jerry said, "Ain't got no problem. I just want to dance with that lady."

He pointed to me and placed a lot of emphasis on the words 'that' and 'lady.' I thought, he meant me and no other woman in the room. He wanted to dance with

THAT lady. The way the word lady rolled off of his tongue and through that big pretty smile made me blush like a six-year old child when somebody tells her she's pretty. I poked my finger in my jaw, smiled real big and started twisting my hair in my fingers.

"No go, partner. You got to wait in line," Jack said.

Jack wouldn't budge, he held me tighter and tighter and we danced until the record stopped. I was...and...was not impressed. Jerry could have started a lot of trouble if I had been dancing with any of my old boyfriends. And, an act like that could have gotten me killed if I had been with Tic. When the record stopped Jack and Jerry stood in the center of the dance floor staring each other up and down.

I pulled Jack close enough to whisper in his ear, "It's just the idea, isn't it?"

Jack stood there staring at Jerry and never even turned to look at me. He said, "Yeah, man. Who the hell he think he is cutting in on my dance?"

I patted Jack on the back and whispered in his ear. "What are you upset about? We're friends, Jack. He probably knows that. I'm sure he saw you here before I got here, and he has probably seen me and Max or Tic and you and Aleena out together."

I could see him relaxing as he thought about what I had just said. He laughed and said, "Yeah, you're probably right." Then he extended his hand to Jerry and said, "Man, I guess it is just the idea you cut in. Ain't a real problem, though. Let me buy you a drink."

"No problem at all. I drink Hennessey and make it a double."

Another record started playing and some guy tried to take my hand to dance. Jerry grabbed my hand and stared into my eyes. "This dance is mine," then he took my other hand out of the other man's hand.

He never took his eyes off of me and I couldn't take my eyes off of him, even though looking up at such a tall man was hurting my neck. He looked into my eyes the entire time, before I knew it he had wrapped his arms around me, almost lifted me off the floor and we were dancing. At that time, he looked very good to me. He was more than a foot taller than me, had the perfect complexion and a smile I had fallen in love with the moment it appeared. I told the other guy I was going to dance with Jerry.

The other guy said, "Well, save the next dance for me, okay?"

"Okay," I said and then I melted into Jerry's arms.

"Okay?" Jerry said, "Are you sure about that? I may want to dance the next record with you. In fact, I may want the rest of the night with you. Don't give away my time, please baby. Spend this time with me." Jerry knew I had been captivated by his smile so he looked into my eyes and flashed another one of those magnetic smiles at me. "They are playing our song. You didn't know we had a song, did you?" he asked with a big smile.

The song was Call Me by Al Greene. Wouldn't you just know it, Call Me just happened to be my most favorite song in the world. I had several favorite songs but that was truly my MOST favorite song. Anything Al sang was my favorite, but Call Me was the crème de la crème. I got lost in the music...moreover; I danced inside of the rhythm of the music. I forgot about Jerry, I was consumed with the soul and sensuality of Al Greene's singing.

I looked up at Jerry with one of those I'm-so-in-love looks I get whenever I hear an Al Greene song. He said something, but I couldn't hear him. The top of my head didn't even touch the bottom of his chin so his words were lost in the space and music.

He bent down and said, "I'm Jerry."

He said something else but I had tuned him out for the sake of the song. When the song was over I said, "It's nice to meet you, Jerry."

"You didn't hear the last part of what I said, did you?"

I didn't have the heart to tell him I tuned him out because he was talking during my favorite song. I simply said, "No? What else did you say?"

"You are going to be my wife," he said with the most sincere look I'd ever seen on a person.

I just knew I had misunderstood what he was saying so I said, "I don't think I heard you this time either. Would you repeat that?"

He repeated, "You are going to be my wife."

I paused for a moment and said, "Now that's an original line. Does it ever work on the women you meet? Or, should I be flattered that you are trying so hard to pull me you said what you think every woman wants to hear? I'm not every woman. I don't want to hear that!"

He laughed out loud and then he repeated it again, "You are going to be my wife."

He had a serious look on his face this time and he looked so deep into my eyes I felt like he was looking inside of me. It made me feel extremely uncomfortable. He would not look away from me. He kept looking into my eyes so often and so deeply the thought occurred to me he might have been looking at his reflection and not me. I pulled away from him but he pulled me back and began looking into my eyes again.

"Are you looking at your reflection in my eyes?"

He looked puzzled and asked, "What kind of drugs are you on?"

I gave him one of those I don't know about you looks. The guy I promised to dance with next sat patiently in the seat at the edge of the dance floor. Two more records played before Jerry let me go. He lifted me from the ground and held me in his arms. Then he kissed me. His lips were soft and hot and I could have easily dropped to the floor from excitement. I tried to act as though it didn't faze me in the least bit. I asked him to put me down and he did. I was trying to pull away from him so I could dance with the other guy but he kept pulling me back into his arms.

"Do you believe in love at first sight?" he asked.

"No," I said and with strength that came from nowhere, I pushed him away from me.

I turned to walk away from him...as far away as I could get.

He grabbed my hand before I could take my first step and said, "Is that it? NO! You are cold … you know that. You could have at least given me an explanation."

He tried to pull me into his arms but I used both hands to push him away and then I took a few steps backward, out of his reach. He looked as though I had hurt his feelings.

He shook his head and smiled at me again and said, "Well, I never believed in love at first sight either until you walk into the room. I've got to have you. You are going to be my wife. I know it. I feel it in my heart; you are already in my soul. You are the one. You are going to be my wife!"

I was both, afraid and flattered but I was more afraid than flattered. I had had bad memories and horrific encounters with men that had made up their minds about me being their wife before. Keep your distance from this guy. I started to say something to him but I decided to keep the thought to myself. He said it again and again. He looked like he was serious and that scared me even more. I thought to myself . . . There is always something wrong with the fine ones. They are either criminals, dumb or lunatics. I looked at him and said, "Yes, of course, I'm going to be your wife. Even though I think you're confusing lust at first sight with love at first sight. They both kinda sound the same, don't you think?"

The next record started playing and he grabbed my hand again and would not let go of it.

"You're wrong, it is love! It's love like I ain't never knew love to be. This is something I ain't never gonna get over. You'll see."

He kept staring at me. I was becoming more and more fearful of him.

He looked me up and down and said, "I like what I'm seeing. You are beautiful and sweet."

"Thanks," I said as I took another step away from him.

He laughed and said, "You can't get away from me if I don't let you go."

The other guy sat there patiently waiting for me to pull away from Jerry but he offered no assistance. I didn't blame him. Jerry was tall and built. The other guy was average build and height. Jack walked over to where we were. He sensed the fear and intimidation I was feeling. He put his hand on Jerry's chest and pushed him back a few steps.

"I hope we ain't got no problems here, partner!" he said.

"Don't make no problems, won't be none," Jerry replied.

Jack put his hand in his coat as if he had a gun in it. He smiled at Jerry and said, "Come on, partner, your drink is getting warm."

They sat down at the table staring at each other the entire time I was on the dance floor. When the record stopped the guy I was dancing with tried to kiss me. Before I knew it, I had pinched and twisted his lips so he couldn't open his mouth. I had his lips locked so tight that a half of, both - his upper and bottom lips, were puffed up and sticking out while the other half was twisted completely to the opposite side of his face. I preached to him about men being pushy and aggressive with women and how his mother never raised him to act that way with women. I was on a high horse and didn't want to come down off of it for a while. He looked remorseful and pensive but he couldn't speak because I held on to his lips while I spoke. After about fifteen seconds I pushed him away. Jerry and Jack were laughing and talking by that time. I didn't know if they had seen what had just happened, but I was glad they didn't react to it.

The next record, Atomic Dog, started playing. I was already mentally and physically exhausted but that was, again, one of my favorite records and I could not pass it up. Jack and Jerry jumped up to dance with me. There was another guy who had asked me to dance while I was dancing with the second guy so I decided to dance with him. I turned to look for him but Jerry grabbed my hand and asked me to sit with him.

"No! Sit on Atomic Dog? Are you out of your mind? Anyway, I told this guy I would dance with him and that's what I'm going to do."

Jerry backed up to his seat and sat down. He stared at me the entire time I was dancing. I never felt so self-conscious in my life. He made me feel like I was doing a private lap dance for him. He sat there clapping and moving his fingers to every hip movement I'd make with every downbeat of the song. I kept dancing around the guy until I was out of Jerry's view. I had finally worked my way to the other side of the room where Jerry could not see me. The next thing I knew, Jerry was dancing with someone right next to me. I kept dancing away from him but he followed me everywhere I went.

Finally, he said, "I've got my eyes on you, girl, you ain't getting out of my sight tonight."

I was nervous and uncomfortable but I smiled and kept on dancing.

CHAPTER FOURTEEN

Thinking about how we met made me realize Jerry always did make me feel uncomfortable and our whole relationship was always about what he wanted. The loud ringing of the phone snapped me back into reality. It disturbed me so much I nervously snatched the phone off the hook and yelled at the person on the other end.

"Hello." Again, it was Jerry. "Jerry, what is it you want?" I snapped.

He wanted to ensure I'd be home by six-thirty. I tried to speak with a civil tone but I just wanted to scream. My only thought was why the heck did you ever approach me in the first place. We had been married for a little more than seven and a half years and I had never been happy with him. I was always uncomfortable and trying to please him.

I said, very calmly, "Yes, I'll be at home at the regular time. We can talk then. Goodbye."

I had just had some pleasant memories of how we got together but hearing his voice made me angry all over again. I had a quick image of his 'perfect' smile with broken, chipped teeth flying out of his mouth as my fist punched it in rapid succession.

I looked up to see Thomas standing at my door staring at me. I wanted to scream, "What now???????????" I wanted to tell him to get out of my office, out of my face, out of my life! That was all I needed at that point - another man who was confused about what he wanted and who wanted to blame everyone else for his confusion. I didn't hate Thomas but I certainly didn't like him. He was an egotistical, arrogant, elitist who felt the world owed him homage because he showed up on the scene.

"Thomas, what is it that you want?" I asked in the most non-threatening voice I could muster. After all, I did work with this man and it looked like I was going to have to learn how to get along with him.

"I really want to talk to you, if you don't mind." He said politely.

Wow, I thought, he's being polite to me. I'd better watch out he's up to something...this man is not to be trusted...no matter how polite he's being.

"Sure," I said, just as politely, "would you like to talk now?"

"Yes, there's something I need to say to you and it can't wait any longer."

"Okay, have a seat. Or, would you prefer to talk in your office or a conference room?" I asked, again being very polite.

"Here is fine."

Thomas walked into my office and closed the door behind him. He pushed the tumbler in to lock the door. I looked at him with a quizzical look on my face and said, "I don't think it is a good idea to close and lock the door, Thomas."

He unlocked the door and walked out. He really was playing cat and mouse and I just didn't have the energy to expend on it. I didn't want to play games.

I went to his office and said, "Look, either we talk out in the open or we don't talk at all. I'm not going to allow you to close doors and lock them when it's only the two of us in the room. If you have something to say to me you either say it in the open or we take it back to Dr. Charles. You are acting like a child, and a spoiled child at that. So, what is it going to be?"

He screamed, "I don't think this is going to work out."

"What, the two of us working together? Is that what you are talking about, Thomas?" I demanded.

"Yes," he shouted. "I don't want to work with you anymore. You ignore me." Then he blurted out, "Why the hell do you stay with him?"

I had no idea of what he was talking about.

"Who, Thomas? Stay with who?"

He grabbed a piece of paper off of my desk and wrote, JERRY!!!!!!!!!!!!!!!

He went on to say, "I'm married myself and I'm not happy but I don't understand why you stay with him? That's all I want to know, why do you stay with him?"

I was flabbergasted and I didn't know what to say to him. I was angry but I held my temper. I spoke very deliberately, "Well, that certainly came out of the blue. I don't quite know how to answer you without telling you to go to hell because my marriage is none of your business."

"Forget it," he shouted. Then he turned and looked at me like everything he loved in the world had been taken away from him. He said, "You know he had an affair with my wife a few years ago."

"No," I said with surprise. "I had no idea that anything like that had taken place."

I thought, finally, I understand now why Thomas hated me so much. He blamed me for introducing them. Hearing what Thomas had to say about Jerry helped me turn the corner from strong dislike to hatred for Jerry.

I was embarrassed and hurt. Knowing Jerry was having an affair with Blascey was bad enough, but knowing I introduced him to a co-worker's wife and he had an affair with her made me hate him even more.

I looked in Thomas' eyes and said, "I had no idea. I can't tell you how sorry and humiliated I feel right now." Then I asked, "Is that why you hate me so much, because Jerry and Martha had an affair?"

He looked at me like I didn't understand anything about life . . . like I was an idiot. "No, I hate them for that. I hate the idea of you being with him."

"Now, I'm confused all over again. I don't understand what you have against me, if it's them you hold responsible for the affair...and, why would it bother you that I'm with Jerry?"

"Forget it." He jumped up to walk out of the room. I walked to the edge of his desk and sat down.

"We've been through enough cat and mouse for one day, Thomas. Come on, I think we can work this out, but we've got to respect each other's boundaries." I turned and walked back to my office and he followed me.

I sat on the edge of my desk and he sat in my seat. And, for the first time in a long time, we talked to each other ... not at each other but to each other. Thomas told me he had come to enjoy and look forward to the mornings we used to sit and drank coffee together. We used to talk about everything under the sun. He said he had never had a happy marriage, and his wife had affairs with a lot of men, every man he knew, in fact. I asked why he didn't divorce her. He looked at me like I was some poor, misguided person who just didn't know anything.

"I've earned my share of her money and I'm not going to see anyone else enjoy the fruits of my labor. I have been through three years of her hell fires and crap and I have really earned my share her money, you better believe it."

I snickered and he smiled. In the next few minutes we were laughing, patting each other on the back and making jokes about how she is now paying for her indiscretions, monetarily. He was actually happy to catch her in the act with Jerry. Before Jerry he had heard rumors and suspected she was having a number of affairs. Jerry was his first real proof. And he was using that situation to his advantage. He said he gone home early one winter day and noticed smoke coming out of the garage. He opened the garage door and there they were, almost knocked out from the carbon monoxide, her head still in Jerry's lap and the two of them sleeping like babies - half dead from the monoxide. He told me the first thing he did was to go into the house to get his camera. He took about thirty pictures of them before he did anything to help them. He thought about leaving them in there but he just couldn't be so cruel. He pushed Jerry and Martha onto the floor. He said Jerry's eyes got as big as buckets and Jerry begged him not to tell me what had happened. He was so angry he threw hot water on them. He offered to bring the pictures in to show me. I assured him it would not be necessary for me to see them.

I felt sorry for Thomas. He was trapped in a marriage without love because of his greed. I realized I was trapped in my marriage because of fear of being alone, obligation and tradition. The tradition in my family was that you stayed with your husband, good or bad. The only thing that would free you was being able to prove your spouse had had an affair. It seemed Jerry was having affairs all over the place so this was my get out of jail free card.

I told Thomas about Jerry and Blascey. Before he realized what he was saying, he blurted out, "Boy, to have a woman like you and to still do wrong. I'd give my eyetooth for you. I really would."

I was shocked and I didn't know what to say. I smiled and said, "Thank you, Thomas, but I'm not comfortable with that kind of talk coming from you."

Making that statement put me right back on his bad side. He felt threatened again. He gave me one of the meanest looks I had seen and stormed out of my office.

"Well, what the hell? "What the hell?" was all I could say.

He slammed the door to his office and in the next minute he was on the phone calling me.

"This is Sarissa," I answered.

Thomas was screaming at this point, "I known damn well who it is, I just called the number. You will regret pushing me away. I'll get you."

All I could think of was the roller coaster ride I'd been on that entire day with him. I hung up the phone while he was talking. I was exhausted from the day's experience with Jerry and Thomas.

CHAPTER FIFTEEN

Within seconds, the phone rang again. I wanted to start pulling my hair out like they do in the movies and scream.   I answered it with the most pleasant tone I could muster. I couldn't say anything nice. All I could say was, "Damn ...Jerry, you again."

This was the third time he had called me that day. I knew something was awfully wrong and he was being manipulated in some way. At any rate, I didn't trust him. I had the distinct feeling I was about to get into a hollering match. I remembered a stress release method I used to do when I took martial arts. I balled my fists as tight as I could and I slowly relaxed and released my hands.   That calmed me enough to talk to Jerry with a civil tone. I saw Thomas coming back toward my office so I quickly walked to the door to shut it. I turned to walk back to my desk but then I decided the only way I'd have any peace was to lock Thomas out so I locked the door. Thomas looked at me and blatantly decided to listen to my conversation. He pressed his face against my window and scooted around until he found a spot where he was comfortable and could best hear my conversation. His face and long curly locks looked like pan-fried meat that had been dried, flattened and overcooked. I decided to ignore him. I was very quiet and calm when I spoke to Jerry. He wanted to know what time I'd be home for the third time and which bus I'd be on. I asked him why and he said he was going to meet me at the bottom of the hill. I told him I catch the No. 6 bus but I didn't want him to meet me. It was the only bus that ran from downtown Cleveland to the City of Euclid and Jerry knew that. I didn't trust Jerry's curiosity. He was trying too hard to ensure I'd be on a certain bus at a certain time. I felt like I was about to fall victim to another one of his attacks.

"Jerry, why are you willing to meet me at the bus stop, tonight?"

He answered in an almost scripted manner; "I don't want you walking up that hill by yourself. It's getting dark early since the time went back."

I held onto the phone and didn't say a word. The silence made him nervous.

He started breathing hard and finally said, "You don't believe me. Or, you don't trust me?"

"Frankly, I don't trust you or believe you. I think you have something up your sleeve and I don't see a good ending in this for you."

"You don't see a good ending in this for me...for me...there won't be a good ending in it for you!" he shouted.

"Well then, don't worry about what time I'll be getting home or what bus I'll be catching and I will see you when I get there."

I could hear him whispering to someone in the background. "She threatened me...what did you expect me to say." Then he returned to the phone and said, "Are you there?"

"Yes I am and I heard every word you just said to Blascey." I heard a click and then dial tone. He had hung up on me again.

I went through the rest of the workday in a fog. I got my work done and even had a few meetings but I couldn't tell you what I did or with whom I had met. I knew I met with Thomas again, but nothing he said held any interest for me. He threatened me, I threatened him, he threatened me again and I threatened him again. Everything else was a blur. I remember re-experiencing Anaghia's movements from inside of her. I could see, very clearly, each person as she moved past him or her. I could feel what they felt. I saw how excited Josephine was from Anaghia's eyes and felt the tinge of jealously Sophie directed toward Anaghia from Sophie's heart. In the next moment I felt the lust and respect Stephen and James felt as she passed them.

I realized I never took the time to get deeply involved in the emotions others had for me. I rationalized that was the reason I was able to stay with Jerry for such a long time. I was not invested in him. I overlooked his contempt for me. I overlooked everything about what he and others felt about me and I had no requirements of him or anyone, at least I'd never made my requirements or expectations known. It wasn't that other people didn't matter to me; it was I didn't feel entitled to go so deeply into another person's feelings.

I wanted to call Anaghia and set up a time to meet so we could run wild through the city like we had the night before. Just as I had that thought, I could see the image of Anaghia's face in front of mine. I was still a bit frightened because I wasn't sure of what was actually happening to me or what had happened. As far as I knew I could have dreamed the whole thing. I wasn't sure if we had run wild through the city at all. In fact, I wasn't sure of anything. The only thing I did feel, with any degree of certainty, was it was quite possible I might have dreamed the entire experience with the wolf. I was torn between my feeling of wanting to know whether or not the experience of the wolf was real and of being afraid of it actually being real. If it were real, that would have meant something was wrong with me. And, if it wasn't real, then something was definitely wrong with me. Either way, something was wrong with me.

I heard doors shutting and voices in the hallway outside of my office. It was the end of the day and it was finally time to go home. What an awful, dreadful thought. I'd have to go back to that place knowing Jerry was waiting for me. But what was he waiting to do? And better yet, if I could become the wolf, what would I do to him? Why was he suddenly so anxious for me to get home? I did hear him whisper to someone. I assumed he was talking to Blascey. Hanging up on me confirmed my belief he was, in fact, talking to Blascey but still I had no real proof. I couldn't really put my finger on anything solid. I needed to think. I needed to be rationale. I sat still and quiet for a while and savored the silence and my solitude.

I closed my eyes and within seconds, I was looking at Jerry and Blascey in a restaurant. They were around the corner at Russo's. Jerry must have started taking Blascey there recently. I had just introduced him to the owners a few months ago. Before he had never even heard of the place. What nerve! He's taking her right around the corner from my job...where everyone I know goes for lunch and after hour entertainment! What a pile of dog poop! I'll be glad to scrape him off the bottom of my shoes.

Both, Blascey and Jerry had on black leather gloves. She took a small bottle out of her purse and said,

"Remember, pour a drop or two in her cup before she pours her cocoa. You got that?"

He looked scared and said, "Yeah. I know what to do with it. I'll rinse her cup for her cocoa and while its wet I'll put a few drops in the cup. She'll pour her own cocoa, so she won't suspect anything. I'll put this vial back in my pocket and I'll drop it out the window where your cousin, Lillian, and her friend, Andrew, will be waiting for the drop. They will pick up the vial and get rid of it."

Blascey nodded in agreement. Lillian and Andrew walked in and sat at the table with them.

Jerry said, "Are you sure there is no way to trace this stuff?"

Blascey was visibly aggravated. She shook her head and growled out the words, "Yes, I am. How many times do I have to tell you, damn?"

Lillian and Andrew had bizarre looks on their faces like they had been drugged.

Lillian said, "What happened to yo' face?"

"Her," Blascey said, as though she was talking to a baby, "She did this to me and she made fun of you two. Called you crazy."

Lillian shook her head so hard her lips hung down and her cheeks shook and flapped opened and closed with every violent turn of her head. Andrew jumped to his feet. His movement was so abrupt and unwarranted he startled everyone at the table.

"What the hell is wrong with you," Blascey blurted out.

Andrew started walking around in circles, mumbling to himself. After about three rounds he said, "She was nice to us last night. She's shy like us. She said she was shy, just like us."

Blascey was very aggravated but she forced a smile and stood up and hugged him. She held the back of his head in her hand and pressed his face into her breast and whispered, "She's an evil woman. She hurt me and made fun of you. That's why we have to teach her a lesson."

Lillian's eyes were almost closed. A tear trickled down the right side of her face as she said, "I thought she liked us. She's evil. We have to teach her a lesson."

Andrew jerked away from Blascey and started shouting, "I don't believe you! She was talking to us. She was nice. She wouldn't make fun of us, she's just like us."

Blascey slapped Andrew and pushed him into the chair at the table, "Look at my face! Take a good look at these bandages all over my face. I had to have one hundred and twelve stitches. Does a nice person try to tear somebody's face apart?"

Andrew would not look at Blascey. He tried to bury his face with his hands. She pulled his hands away from his face and moved even closer to him as she angrily said, "Nice people don't try to kill other people. Nice people don't tear other people's faces apart."

Lillian opened her mouth but didn't say anything.

Blascey snapped out the words, "What do you have to say. Just say it, okay. Say whatever is on that small mind of yours, Lillian!"

Lillian sat back in the chair and gave Blascey one of those looks that seemed to question everything she had just said, and then she blurted out, "Then why we trying to kill her if nice people don't try to kill other people?"

There weren't many people in the restaurant but everyone who was there stopped talking and turned their attention to Blascey, Jerry, Lillian and Andrew.

Jerry jumped out of the seat and quickly left the restaurant.

Blascey looked around the room at everyone and screamed, "Excuse us, my niece is auditioning for a part in a play and she just spoke too loud. I'm sure you all know how that is so please enjoy your meals and disregard what you just heard."

Lillian shouted just as loud, "I ain't auditioning for a part in no play! You are a liar, Blascey. You are a big liar and I don't believe what you telling me."

Blascey was now upset with Andrew, Lillian and Jerry. She tried to calm Lillian but Lillian stood up and screamed, "I ain't gonna help you hurt her, she is my friend. She is just like us. Shy!"

Blascey grabbed Lillian's arm and snatched Andrew's shirt and pulled him out of his seat. She pushed them toward the restaurant door.

The waitress ran after her and said, "You owe $37.60 for your bill, Miss."

"Give it to my friend when he comes back, "Blascey snapped.

"I can't do that, Ma'am."

"Well, hell, we got a problem because I ain't giving you nothing. I have enough problems trying to get these two dummies to..."

Blascey stopped suddenly and tried to retract her words. "I didn't mean that, I'm just mad."

Lillian pulled away from her and Andrew pushed her away from him. The waitress stood in front of the door and blocked the exit.

"Miss, if you don't pay your bill it will come out of my salary and I can't afford that. So, I need $37.60 from you now."

Blascey pushed her way past the waitress and was half way out the door when she felt the button on her high collared blouse pressing against her throat so hard she began to gag.

"We can do this the easy way or the hard way, Miss. Frankly, I don't care which way it goes. So, what's it going to be?" the waitress asked in an irritated voice.

"The thing is," said Blascey, "I am tired of getting the short end of the stick. Why should I pay when he is the one who ate? I'll pay you for what I ordered and they didn't have anything so let him come back and pay for his part."

Blascey's face was next to the doorframe when the blunt force of the waitress' fist slammed into it. The punch sounded so loud it shattered the vision and shocked me back into reality.

CHAPTER SIXTEEN

I had been having strange visions my entire life so I could not put any stock into what I had seen or was seeing at any moment. I left my office to catch the bus to go home. As I turned the corner I saw the bus pulling off. I decided to walk. It was a ten-mile walk but it was a straight shot so I didn't mind. I passed Thomas' car three times within a half mile from the office. I was nearing an abandoned factory with a few abandoned cars in the parking lot. The parking lot had big chunks of broken glass and a few chalk outlines where dead bodies were found. I slowed down so I could assess my surroundings. I looked into the pitch-black rooms that loomed behind the huge, broken factory windows. I saw shadows moving in the blackness. Hot, piercing streams of energy moved over my body and burned me like a fire-lit branding iron. My vision became crystal clear. I could see inside the buildings and miles down the street. I felt my body strengthening and began looking through round yellow orbs. The heat started to dissipate as I moved closer to the building. The transformation never completed, though. Before I knew it, I had transformation back into myself. I walked without fear and I watched everything around me with a newfound interest. The old abandoned factory with the black rooms seemed somewhat artistic. I thought about coming back one day to sketch the building in pen and ink. I wondered what had happened to the people who used to live there. Where were they? How did this building and this section of town get so worn down? I looked at the outlines of the bodies on the ground and wondered who had witnessed their destruction and why they had been killed. I wondered about their souls and their spirits…were they still wondering the earth or had they moved into a different dimension of life? I wondered about the people who waited for them to come home and the sadness they must have felt when they never returned to them. My mind was filled with morbid thoughts about how and why those people were killed. I began to question, under what circumstances I would be willing to kill. Tearing Blascey's face open didn't affect me in the way I would have thought. I had no remorse for hurting her. I wondered if

I would have killed her and I wondered why I had not when I knew she was trying to kill me.

I could hear the engine of a car speeding up the street, while at the same time, I felt negative, intense heat directed at me. This heat scorched me from the back. It was fiercely intense. I stopped moving and stood perfectly still for a few seconds. I gauged the intervals of heat dispersion to be intense but shielded by something. I lowered my head and turned to look behind me. Thomas' car was behind me and he was driving erratically and every few seconds he'd stick his head of out the window and yell at me. Actually, he screamed at me the entire time . . . ordering me to get into his car. I refused to ride with him. He pulled away from me several times. Each time he would press the gas pedal so hard the car would screech and burn the rubber on the wheels. And, each time he would return and begin screaming out of his window at me again. Thomas was angry and I felt every bit of his anger as it increased. It cut me like hot spikes and the hot fiery waves of energy pierced my back, shoulders and neck. His car was half way on the street the other half was on the sidewalk. He was about to run me over and I knew it. He picked up speed and bumped me with his car. I asked him to stop but he kept right on bumping me. Each time he would bump me harder and harder. The snout I longed to see was finally in front of me, snarled and wiggling to an eight/eight beat as deep hard growls rolled from the back of my throat through my tight, clinched teeth. I saw saliva drip off of long, white, sharp fangs and hit the ground and I felt strength and courage surge throughout my entire body as I moved. I looked back at Thomas, who was now rubbing his eyes so hard I could hear a sound each time he would twist the ball of his fists in his eyes. A broken down car that had been emptied from the inside out stood a few feet in front of me. I lowered my head to the ground, pushed back on my hind legs and leapt on the car in front of me. I turned around just as the hood of Thomas' car was next to the hood of the broken down car. In a flash I had jumped from the hood of the broken down car onto the hood of Thomas' car. Thomas stopped his car abruptly and my hind legs slid around on the hood but my long claws clung onto the rim of the hood next to the window in front of the driver's seat. Thomas blew the horn hoping someone in that abandoned part of the city would come to his rescue. With the force of a tank I thrashed long, sharp claws into the hood, tearing open the metal hood like it was a sheet of paper. Thomas reached into his glove compartment and pulled out a gun. He pulled out a small box of bullets but he was so nervous he could not load the gun. All of the bullets fell onto the seat and the floor.

At that moment, I knew the enemy was upon me and I had to fight to preserve my life. Up until that moment I saw Thomas as a man and I understood everything that was going on around me as a woman, yet I had transformed into the wolf. I could feel cold and hot streams of energy coming at me. Thomas was confused, scared and angry. In his confusion, he got out of the car. I struck him with my paw as soon as his foot touched the ground. The force of the blow was so powerful he was knocked a foot into the air. He landed on the ground next to a big rock. He grabbed a big chunk of glass and started swinging wildly and aimlessly in the air. I stepped back to watch him for a few seconds. After linking into his rhythm I lunged at him and pinned his arms onto the ground. He was still angry. His energy was still hot and it burned me. I leaned down close to his face and growled in victory. I growled until he stopped twisting and turning. He stopped moving and lay perfectly still but his energy was still hot. He was trying to trick me into walking away but his energy told me a different story. His energy identified him as an enemy-at-large; an enemy whose sole purpose at the time was to kill me if I didn't kill him. He was my enemy and he was pinned securely against the ground, incapable of harming me. I turned my head sideways so I could get a good grip on his neck. I saw my long, sharp, glistening fangs and a snarled, twisted snout as I opened my mouth wide enough to bite and tear his neck apart. Suddenly, his hot energy turned cold. I knew then he was afraid and would no longer pose a threat to my existence. Still I placed my fangs on either side of his neck and I lightly applied pressure until my fangs gently sunk into the veins that protruded from his neck. I pressed until I felt drops of Thomas' blood touch my tongue. I opened my mouth wide, releasing him from my grip, and backed away from him. I was not hungry and no longer in danger so I saw no need to kill him. He and I, both, knew I had that option and could exercise it at any time, so I let it go.

As Thomas tried to lift himself from the ground, he put his hand into his pocket and tried to pull something out of it. Still, not fearing for my life, I knew Thomas needed to have the strongest warning possible so he would stop trying to hurt me before he got killed. As he pulled his hand out of his pocket and out from under his jacket pocket, I bit him, taking a big plug out of his arm. Then I pushed him with my head until he was pinned against the car. His arm bled profusely and every time he looked down at it, he held his head as though he was about to faint. I growled out a warning for him to get back in his car and drive away. He stood there staring at me. His immobility was not due to an inability to move, it was his stubbornness. I moved so close to him he could not move. I stood on my hind legs and stared straight into his eyes. For a brief second he looked back into my eyes as though he was issuing a challenge to me. I growled and opened my mouth until my fangs were touching the top of his head and the bottom of his chin. I wanted him to know I was not one to be threatened or taken lightly. I could hear the urine hit the ground and Thomas' shoes as I lowered my body to the ground and backed away from him. He stumbled and got back into his automobile. In the next second, I heard a loud screeching sound, smelled burning gases and watched his car speed down Euclid Avenue away from me.

The shadows behind the broken factory window moved back and forth the entire time I had my encounter with Thomas. The energy that came from the figures behind the broken windows became hotter as I moved closer to the factory. These creatures were familiar to me. I understood their nature intimately and could predict their actions. They howled out a warning to let me know they were there. They had marked off the boundaries of their territory with urine. The howling was to inform all who wandered into their territory that the rules of engagement were established and would be dictated by the alpha male. As the wolf, I didn't solicit confrontation and I didn't run from it. I didn't care that I was in what they thought was their territory. The shadows leaped out of the windows and became clear images. They looked like me but they were very different.

They were weak and insignificant but not like the creatures I had encountered earlier. They were not canis they were canine - weak street dogs. They moved constantly around the perimeter but they never moved toward me. They went in the opposite direction. I embraced the night air and the challenges that lay ahead. As I past the factory I transformed back to myself. I was in somewhat of a daze. I realized I had been inside of the wolf and I could taste Thomas' blood in my mouth.

Even though I had transformed back to myself everything about me had been enhanced and it stayed that way. My vision was perfect; my sense of touch, hearing and taste had all been enhanced since becoming the wolf a few minutes earlier. I could not only smell the gases in the air but I could taste remnants of gases and the foods that filled the air from restaurants a mile away. I was enjoying the beauty of the dark sky, the stars and the cool of the night. I felt strong and in control. I had no fears as I walked home. A long stretch of Euclid Avenue was populated with businesses; clubs and restaurants so there were a lot of people out walking around. I walked about four miles before I reached the residential area.

I saw a small sports car pass me with the license plate MYTURN. It was speeding down the street and Jerry was behind the wheel. I watched him dart through traffic for at least another mile. Blascey, Lillian and Andrew were in the car too. Andrew saw me as they sped by. He stared and smashed his face against the back window. He pointed at me and I could hear him whispering to himself.

"She made fun of us. We have to teach her a lesson."

I whispered back, "Don't be fooled by Blascey and Jerry. They want you to hurt me. I wouldn't make fun of you or anyone else. We shy people should stick together, not hurt each other."

I could see him jump up and down in his seat, bumping his head on the roof of the car. He tried to tell Blascey and Jerry what he had just heard me say but they dismissed it.

CHAPTER SEVENTEEN

I had never felt more free and fearless than I had walking home that night. I knew I would never be helpless or a victim again. The air was cold and brisk but I was hot. Heat and strength surged throughout my body. I could hear my heartbeat in my ears and see the snout in front of my face. I was happy to embrace the wolf again, and I hoped to do battle. I saw no immediate danger so I frolicked in the night air. I ran and played for what seemed like hours. I jumped up to bite leaves and branches of the trees, I stretched my paws out and scratched up piles of dirt and grass and I chased cars as they sped past me. I jumped up at the stars in the sky and I watched the stars as though they were pictures of familiar sights. Dark figures moved in big clouds away from the moon. It was a full moon that night. It was like a bright, beautiful, glowing round burst of energy that stared at me from the heavens and guided my every step.

My playful mood stopped abruptly. My instinct to preserve my life was upon me again. Three streams of negative, intense heat disturbed the cold, brisk, air and reached me within a few seconds. The heat encircled my entire body and narrowed to three distinct points - my neck, ribs and right hind leg. This meant there were three creatures ready to attack me. Their energy was much more intense than my earlier encounters with the human creatures. I knew the nature of these creatures and I could smell the strong scent of canine in the air. I slowed my joyful prance to a staunch, deliberate gait. I lowered my head almost to the ground so I could gage the intensity and strength of the canine. I could gage their strength by the amount of heat present and its closeness to the ground. With my head still close to the ground, I turned my head, slowly, from side to side. Squinting my eyes brought the image of two of the canine immediately into view. The energy that emanated from them was weak in comparison to the force of energy that came from behind me. Still weak, the energy from all three intensified as they moved closer to me. The canine behind me was the biggest of the three but it was nowhere near strong enough to present a challenge to my strength. Two thirds of the heat generated came from him so he would be the one I'd attack first. The two on the sides of me were not strong at all. They were hungry and weak. Their energy reached me in kilocycles, which meant these creatures were skinny, and didn't have much meat on their bodies to block or slow the cycle speed of the electric energy. Their apparent lack of food caused them to be even more inferior, an adversary, than they would have been naturally. The heat from their bodies hit me in cycles, weak cycles. They were hungry and became weaker by the minute. They were waiting for their alpha male to attack and pin me down. His energy struck me on the neck and that would be his point of attack. He was also weak and hungry so he would have strength in his teeth from his great desire for food but his ability to stabilize the bite and pull me down would be weakened by unsteady legs and a weak neck. He was planning to attack me from the back so I'd turn and lunge at him, knocking the breath out of him and then I'd tear his throat out. The other two would run. Only after I'd leave the scene would they come back and get the nourishment off of him they wanted to get off of me. Collectively, they would have been worthy opponents if they had been healthy and strong but they were weak and inferior. I knew there would be nothing they could do to win the battle against me. The weaker two were becoming more fearful as time went on, but their desire for food overpowered their fear. The alpha male had no choice but to attack me.

When I turned to face the alpha male he stopped approaching me because he realized I was canis and not canine. He realized he had no win with me. His energy cycled between hot and cold, aggression and fear. The alpha male knew I was much more than he...in stature and stamina...and I realized he had no choice but to attack. They were starving and there were no food alternatives available. Within seconds the hair on my shoulder blades, back and neck was wet, standing straight up and apart. New strength saturated me. My heart was beating stronger and louder in my ears, my claws were stretched forth and my long, sharp teeth were in view and dripping with saliva. The edges of my mouth were taunt, pulled back and stretched tight from one end to the other, my nose flared and pulled heaps of the cold night air in through my nostrils and into my strong lungs. My eyes were almost closed tight and focused on my opponents. I had all three of them in view.

I moved toward the alpha male. I smelled the remnants of blood and could see he had an old wound on his neck, one that had not yet healed. That would be my striking point. My powerful hind legs would power my lunge and I'd knock him to the ground. I would hold him down and sink my teeth into his neck until he bled to death. These canines were shabby, weak, city creatures that didn't know how to survive. The alpha male barked and growled and showed his teeth as I moved closer to him. I heard a deep, resonating growl that shook my entire body come from inside of me. I felt rage build within me as I moved closer and closer to my targets. The alpha male barked and backed up as I moved closer. The other two were barking and growling yet their energy continued to dissipate. Their energy was neutralizing, that meant they were becoming more fearful. The energy of the alpha male continued to cycle between hot and cold and it burned and chilled me as I moved toward him. Suddenly I felt a hot negative energy come from behind me. It was the energy of another canis. This time it was not directed toward me, it passed over me and hit the alpha male. The alpha male's energy began to neutralize and suddenly became cold. He was in fear. He growled and barked and the three canines ran down the street together, screeching and squealing, as though they had already been defeated in the attack.

I knew I was no longer in danger of attack so I turned to greet my friend of the other night. We ran, fast, up the street, chasing cars and playing along the way. As I reached the corner of Superior Hill and Euclid Avenue my friend turned to go back down Euclid Avenue while I went up Superior Hill. I took a few steps and looked back. My friend was not there but a large, beautiful nighthawk swooped close to my head and flew straight up into the sky. I watched it until it disappeared into the dark clouds that moved across the sky. I heard a noise as I passed the parking lot with the store and bar where I had encountered the other two human creatures. The noise was shrill and it came from the little sports car with the license plate that read MYTURN that was parked in front of the entrance to the bar. There were four humans inside of it. They were large but apparently very weak. I could see no usefulness in them. They must have been designated as a new kind of food. I was ever mindful, though, of the dangerous instrument that held the lightening bolts these humans possessed.

The human that got out of the car was large and it moved quickly toward me. It didn't emit the negative, hot energy that aggressively challenged me or the cold, brisk energy that indicated a fear of me. Regardless, I stopped to ready myself for an attack. I watched as it moved thoughtlessly toward me. It was then I realized it didn't see me. This human was oblivious to my presence and anything else around it. Perhaps because it was so large it had no reason to feel threatened by, or fear others. It began to run in my direction. I knew I was not in danger so I began a slow, steady walk up the hill. After a few minutes it saw me and stopped moving. I immediately felt the cold icy waves of energy its body emitted. I stood there watching it walk backwards to the little sports car. Even though my understanding of life had been enhanced after my encounter with Blascey, and I could distinguish one human creature from another, I still didn't understand the sounds humans made. The large human banged on the window and emitted high-pitched, screechy noises that disturbed me. As soon as he got into the car, white lights in the front of the car and red lights on the back of the car lit up and the car sped away.

I reached the Superior Hill Towers much quicker than I wanted. The apartment management had just installed three sets of floodlights on each side of the building. They had a complaint of some strange animals lurking around the building so they figured the lights would keep the animals at bay. What strange rationale they used. If the animals were creatures like themselves perhaps the lights would deter them. But, if the animals were wild like me the lights would attract them. I moved forward, closer to the building. The lights just brightened the pathway for me to see everything better. As my foot touched the driveway pavement I felt a transformation come upon me. I felt physically weak and fragile but my confidence and spirit were strong. Even though I dreaded going into my apartment I knew I was about to enter a new phase of my life and I welcomed an end to the charade Jerry and I had gone through for so many years.

I was becoming more certain about what was going on with the wolf. The visions I had of Jerry and Blascey were strange but they were also very clear and they had nothing to do with the wolf, as far as I knew. Still, I had had visions before that seemed significant but ended up meaning absolutely nothing and I had had visions that seemed insignificant but held a great deal of meaning, direction and value for me later in life. I decided to go into the back entrance so I could get a soda before going to my apartment. From the parking lot I looked up at the dark sky but I was distracted by the fact that there were lights on in every room of my apartment. I stood quietly and watched for a while. I could see Jerry running from the kitchen to the bathroom, to the bedroom, and back to the kitchen again. He sat down at the counter for a few minutes and then he walked quickly back into the bathroom. The window was opened in the bathroom and I watched him rinse his face several times. The only thing I could surmise from his actions was he was nervous.

My friend, Pam, greeted me as I entered the building. She was out of breath. Her baby was strapped into one of those baby carriers on her back and she had a basket of laundry she was struggling to carry back to her apartment. We got on the elevator and I got off at her floor. I took the basket and walked her to her apartment.

She said, "You're early, I'm glad I saw you. I was going to leave out in another five minutes to pick you up at the bus stop. I had a million and one things to do first but I was going to pick you up for sure. I just don't like the idea of you walking up that hill at night."

I assured her I didn't need a ride. I made it seem like I had met someone on the bus I was interested in.

She looked a little disappointed but then shrugged her shoulders and said, "Well, I can't say I'm not aware of something going on with Jerry and that woman who tried out for your troupe."

"What woman?"

I could tell she felt like she had just let the cat out of the bag on Jerry.

"I thought you knew...the other day, you sent them out of the apartment with Robert. Oh, I'm so sorry, I thought you knew."

I assured her she had done no harm by mentioning the woman. I didn't remember Blascey trying out for my troupe. More than likely I had nothing to do with the selection process whenever she had tried out. I could see Pam was uncomfortable talking about Blascey to me but I questioned her anyway.

"I know about Jerry and this woman, Blascey, but I don't remember Blascey trying out for Panache."

"Oh, I don't know how you could forget her," she exclaimed. "I remember it as clear as day. After your rehearsal about a year ago she waited for you and wanted you to explain to her why she wasn't asked to go to your Callback table. She had come the week before and was not on the callback list either. You said something to her and walked away. She was angry and grabbed your arm and turned you around. You don't remember that?"

The memory of that day flooded my mind in seconds. "Yes," I said. "I do remember her now and I couldn't tell her why she wasn't selected then because I didn't take part in the selection process."

Pam continued, "Oh, she ranted and raved on how she was going to humiliate you and make you feel the same pain she felt. When she ran through the revolving door her heel got caught. It broke off and she fell. Her dress was wrapped around her head. It was humiliating. You tried to help her but she kicked at you." Sophie helped her up and you know how Sophie is, she sort of pushed her out the door. Jerry was outside and he talked to her for a long time. I can never forget that day."

Suddenly, everything made a lot better sense. Blascey was getting revenge by taking Jerry away from me. I laughed at the thought of her thinking she's getting even with me by trying to take him. She could have made some money to take him off of my hands because I would have paid her to do it. She could not have done me a bigger favor in life. She had no idea of the kind of hell she was about to bring down on herself. I wanted out of the marriage with Jerry in the first month.

I left Pam and walked one floor up to my apartment. I released a long sigh and opened the door to my apartment. Jerry ran into the living room and flopped down onto the sofa. The pillows on both sides of him were just resettling as I opened the door. He had beads of sweat on his forehead and a big grin on his face. He looked very strange to me. His eyes were glazed and he had the same look Lillian and Andrew had on their faces. I knew Jerry liked to drink alcohol but I had never known him to take any drugs and I had the distinct impression Jerry had been taking drugs. I walked into the bedroom and sat on the bed. He walked to the bedroom door and stood there. The dazed looked turned from a stupid, simple look to one of concern and heartache. Looking at him standing in that door reminded me of how he was when we first got together. I shook my head so that I would snap out of that sympathetic mode.

"Jerry, what's on your mind?"

He reached out for me to hug him and said, "I don't want us to break up. I don't care what has gone on in the past twenty-four hours. I love you and I want to be with you."

I felt a tinge of sympathy but not enough to trust him. I tried to force an understanding smile at him but all I could manage was a grimacing nod. When I looked at him, I saw the image of Martha with her face in his crouch and Blascey giving him a bottle of what I believed to be poison to kill me with.

"I think it's a little late, Jerry. Things have been sour between us a lot longer than twenty-four hours don't you think?" I looked at him and callously said, "Anyway, I don't have any feelings for you and I don't want to continue living like this. I certainly can't say I love you."

"Well, I don't really love you either but I think we can learn to love each other, don't you?"

"Not after seven and a half years," I chided. "What did you want to tell me, Jerry? Was it that you didn't want us to break up? Or, was it something else?"

He was angry, I could tell but he tried not to show it.

"You want something to drink? You normally drink hot cocoa when you get home don't you?"

"Yes," I said hesitantly. "I drink hot cocoa when I get home every night. It's nice of you to notice."

A deep funk came over me. I was so disappointed in Jerry I didn't know what to do. I thought I'd better wait to see if he gives me an empty cup. The phone rang and he ran to it to grab it.

He looked at me and said, "I'll get it," but I had already picked up the receiver. As soon as I said hello the phone went dead.

"Either it is the wrong number or it's Blascey calling to remind you to wash the cup first so the liquid in your little vial, there, will blend in with the water that you rinse the cup with. That way I'll never suspect anything. And don't forget, I'm supposed to pour the cocoa myself."

I looked up at the door where Jerry was standing but he wasn't there. In the next second I heard the front door slam shut. I assumed from his reaction, my vision was accurate. It was hard to swallow the fact he actually was trying to kill me. Or, was I scaring him and just jumping to conclusions. Whatever that was in the jar, he was planning to use it on me just like Blascey had instructed him. I felt Jerry's passion when he said he loved me. He lied when he said he didn't love me. He was embarrassed by my response and he wanted to hurt me. Anyway, at all costs, he sincerely didn't want us to break up. I felt his energy and his sincerity in my heart as he spoke. I realized how much of a mess he had gotten himself in with Blascey. Even though he was constantly listening to her raving about killing me, it wasn't really sinking in with him because he vacillated between wanting us to start anew and killing me because I disappointed him. I realized, too, how I had just turned him back to her and she could continue to manipulate and guide his every step. I knew then I'd have to talk to Jerry. He desperately needed someone to help him wake up before it was too late, before he forced me to hurt him.

CHAPTER EIGHTEEN

I locked the door and went into my bedroom. I was on the edge of my bed in a trance-like state staring out into the beautiful, bluish-black sky. Again, I saw the figure of a large bird with a very, very wide wingspan coming toward my room. The large nighthawk landed on my banister. Still, I sat there almost mesmerized, glaring at the nighthawk and the beauty of the night, itself. The mattress sunk down next to me and squeaked. I turned to see Anaghia sitting next to me on the bed. I could not stop looking at the beauty of the darkness of the night. I spoke in a soft, modulated tone, almost in a whisper.

"Thank you for coming, tonight."

"I will always come when you need my help," she replied.

"I'm confused, Anaghia. I don't know what is real anymore," I said with tears rolling down my face.

"It's all real," she said empathetically, "It doesn't matter when or how it happens. It happens! Do not concern yourself with whether it is in your dreams or when you are awake. What happens in your dreams is just as true and real as the things that happen when you are awake. The experience is real either way."

She was right. It was real to me. The experience was so real I could not distinguish between a dream and reality.

"Are you really here with me right now?" I asked.

"I am never away from you," she replied, "Do you remember when you were thirteen years old. You had a dream."

I turned to look at her but it felt like I was turning in slow motion, when in fact, it was a lightning fast reaction.

"I had a dream that started when I was thirteen but didn't end until I was twenty."

She spoke very softly with almost a musical rhythm to her words, "The dream ended each night you dreamed it but you dreamed it every year for seven years. When you were thirteen you were called to a great challenge. You were in great danger. You were being prepared for battle. You were one of the few spirits to survive the attacks. When you were thirteen three men raped you and you survived the rape but they killed your spirit. When you entered this world, it was known then you were a person who would experience much conflict and endure many battles. It was also known you were a person who could win these battles. You were directed and led to be the person you are today. The spirit of canis greeted you in your dreams to restore your spirit and strengthen your character. Do you remember the dream? Go back ... remember. In the end, it will only help you."

"I am reminded of it every September 23rd and every time I see anything about wolves on television. I could never forget that dream because it stayed there, unresolved in my mind. I never knew the significance of it. I never knew how to find meaning in the wolves or the fact that moments after the dream began, I was the only human in the dream."

"It would be difficult for you to discern on your own. I have been sent here to help you understand. I am your shaman, your interpreter and your ancestor...my blood runs hot in your veins. I will help you clarify the events of your life. "

I was just wondering why you had come to help me. Do you know all of my thoughts?

Yes, and you also know mine. Remember the dream. It is significant. Remember the dream.

I could never forget that dream. I had the exact same dream on the exact same night, September 23rd, each year for seven years. And, each year on September 24th I'd wake up cold, shivering, wet and exhausted from the activities that took place in the dream the night before.

In the dream, I was walking home from school and thinking about the dreadful event that took place a few months earlier, on my thirteenth birthday. I was feeling humiliated and ashamed. I could see people in houses and working in their yards until I reached East 143rd Street.   After that, there were no people...just wolves and me.

East 143rd Street was the place I had always believed to be the entrance into my neighborhood. It was also the street the three guys who raped me walked me down, with a gun in my back and a knife to my throat. It felt like the longest street in the world on that day . . . my thirteenth birthday.

Those guys dared me to run and I guess the mere fact they were as bold as they were and carried a gun - their audacity - must have dared anyone to try to help me.

I could see curtains pulled back and heads bobbing up and down watching me as I was being marched down the street. Everybody was peeping at me, knowing those guys would just as well kill me than let me go. Not only did my neighbors not come out to help me, they never called for help for me. One of my neighbors did stop her car. She was not fearful of the men or the weapons they had. She looked at me with so much disgust in her face I hung my head in shame. She shook her head in disapproval as though I had gotten caught doing something I had no business doing. I pleaded with her to call the police. Her reply hurt me worst than being marched down the street and later being raped.

She smiled and said, "Those boys are just playing with you."

Then she rolled up her window and drove slowly down the street. I looked up to see her eyes staring at me with hopeful anticipation in them. And she drove slowly enough for her eyes to paint a painful picture that would stay in my mind for the rest of my life. I was confused by her words and actions. I had hoped she was saying such harsh words to throw them off track. The passing of time and the lack of any policemen showing up proved she just didn't care. She wanted them to hurt me. She wanted something really awful to happen to me...maybe even death! I never did figure her out. Why she would want something so awful and potentially dangerous to happen to a thirteen-year-old girl. I thought she liked me. I thought I was like a second daughter to her. That's what she always told me. But, the gleam in her eye somehow said I deserved what was about to happen to me. Other people passed me in their cars and shook their heads with fear and disapproval at the boys but they never stopped to help. I didn't think I had a right to blame them because helping me could have meant they would be intimidated, hurt or killed.

My parents were at work and my brother, Toot, was only eight years old. I was going to have to live with the shame of what they were about to do to me for the rest of my life. I marched down the middle of that street with cars swerving and swaying around me, trying not to hit me. I prayed one would stop and let me get in and then speed away, or one would hit the men that were marching me down that street, and finally, I prayed one would hit me so hard I'd die before my body could hit the ground.

One of the men was a neighbor named Matthew. He moved into our neighborhood about two year before that happened. The other two were outsiders who visited him all of the time. The one who initiated this attack on me was twenty-one years old. His name was Donald. The other was another friend of Matthew's from his old neighborhood. They were members of a gang in the village called the Farm Hand Boys. Donald liked me the first time he met me and he tried to get me to date him. I was only eleven when I met him and boys were the last things on my mind. I had to fight every day with the boy across the street, Lester, for the stupidest reasons. He picked on me relentlessly. We have a push and punch fight just about every night for two years straight.

The first time I saw Donald he was sitting in his car in front of Matthew's house. I was there to play with Matthew's sister, Dwanna. She and I were running away from her little brother, Justin. I was looking back as I ran around the side of the house. I didn't look up or forward in time enough to see Donald's car parked in the driveway and I ran into it. I heard him curse as my body hit the bumper. I fell back from the thrust and hit my head so hard I was knocked out. When I opened my eyes Donald was standing over me. He had very pretty eyes. I would have never guessed such destruction and disregard for others could lie behind such beautiful, soft eyes. They were big and brown and his lashes were long and luscious. He had the kind of lashes women dreamed of and could only find in the cosmetics section of a fine department store or high-scale salon.   He picked me up and sat on the porch steps. He forced me to sit in his lap. I felt stupid being cradled like a baby so I tried to get up. He held me tight and rocked back and forth.

"I'm okay. I can get off of your lap now?"

He scooted me around so I faced him and he positioned me so my face was directly in front of his. He held me tighter and said, "Do you believe in love at first sight?"

I was shy and scared and I didn't know what to say.

He asked again, "Do you believe in love at first sight?"

"I don't know." I said as I struggled to get up. He kissed me on my cheek but it was so close to my mouth that a part of his lips touched mine. I couldn't believe it. I was scared and excited. This was the first time I'd been kissed on the lips by a boy. He let me get up but he wouldn't let me move away from him. He held my hand and forced it down by my side while he brushed me off. I looked at the ground the whole time he held me there. I was so embarrassed and scared that all I could do was look down at my feet. Lester and some of his friends were walking down the street. He saw me standing next to Donald and he ran over to us and pushed Donald away from me.

"What happened to you?"

"I ran into his car and I fell down," I said in a soft, scared voice.

He lifted my face and made me look at him. "You are so dumb. How you run into a car? Go home and clean yo'self up, you stupid thing." He yanked my arm and pushed me down the driveway.

I cried from shame and embarrassment and ran home. After about a half and hour I walked out onto my porch. To my surprise, Donald was sitting on my porch waiting for me.

"You didn't have to come to see about me."

"I know. I was just making sure you were okay."

I smiled and sat down beside him. "I'm going back to play with Dwanna is she still at home?"

He didn't answer me. "Your father wouldn't let me come in to see you. I told him I was coming to court you."

"You was coming to do what?"

"I want to court you," he replied as he took my hand and kissed it.

"I don't know what courting is but if it is having boyfriends, I can't have none. I'm only eleven years old."

"You only eleven!" He said with great surprise.

"I know, I'm tall for eleven." I said shyly.

"No. You are built like a woman and you are too beautiful to be eleven."

He looked me and up down. I couldn't look at him. I bit my fingernails and twisted my hair up in a knot. I was completely shy and I felt totally uncomfortable.

"How would you like to have a secret boyfriend?"

I looked across the street at Lester as he walked from behind his house with Dwanna. My heart sank about a foot and a half. He took my face in his hands and turned it so I looked him squarely in his eyes and said, "When you grow up, I'm going to marry you. What you think about that?"

I smiled shyly and looked away from him as I spoke. "I don't know what to think about that. I think you too old for me. You almost a man, I'm just eleven."

When I looked at him he moved close to kiss me but I moved away from him. I looked at my door to make sure that my stepfather was not in the doorway or close enough to the door to see what Donald had just tried to do.

He asked again, "What do you think about marrying me when you grow up? We don't even have to wait. Hell, I'll marry you now!"

I shrugged my shoulders, covered my face with my hands and closed my eyes. When I opened them, Lester and Dwanna were standing there too.

"What y'all want?" Donald asked and then he continued, "Lester, did y'all do it?"

"Yeah, we did it," Lester replied.

Dwanna stood there with a stupid grin on her faced that went from one side to the other.

"Did what?" I asked.

Lester started to dance around and sing. "We just did the p-u-s..." but I interrupted him and said.

"You did it with her?"

His face turned serious and he said, "Yeah, cause I'm saving you for later. You will be my gift on our wedding day! You will be my present to myself."

Donald jumped to his feet and hollered, "What you talk'n bout? I'm gonna marry her when she grows up. The minute she turns eighteen we getting married. You got dat!"

I could tell Lester wanted to argue with him but he just decided to let it slide. He looked at me with contempt in his eyes. He balled his fists and turned to

Donald. Dwanna licked her tongue at me and I got up quickly and turned to walk into the house. I had a sick feeling in my stomach. She had a stupid look on her face. Lester pushed her over toward Donald and spit on the ground.

"Gone man, it's yo' turn."

Donald grabbed my hand before I could open the door and said, "I'm gonna marry you so I want you to stay a virgin. I'll be finished with her in about ten minutes then I'll be back to see you, okay?"

"No," I shouted, "I don't want you to come back to see me."

"Okay, then I won't go with her now. I won't go, okay."

"Go!"

"No, I won't if it's going to make you mad at me."

"I don't want you to ever come around me, so go with her. Go now."

"You're just mad. I won't go. I'll be back to see you tonight, okay." He still had my hand. He kissed each of my fingers and then he let my hand go.

I didn't say anything I just walked into the house. A few minutes later my mother walked into the house. Lester was with her, telling her how nice she looked and that he had seen her earlier that day at work. He sat on the sofa next to me and I got up and went upstairs to my room. He went back out on my porch where he and Donald stayed for most of the day.

Donald never gave up over the next year. He came by to see me every other day and Lester fought with me every single day for something stupid. On my twelfth birthday Donald gave me a diamond ring. I showed it to my stepfather and he made me give it back.

"You going to a convent!" were his only words.

From that day on he was on a crusade to get me into a convent. I did give the ring back to Donald and I told him I couldn't have diamonds or a real ring. I had no intentions of marrying Donald but I was flattered he paid so much attention to me. I was so young and he was already a man. He was a very good-looking man that a lot of women wanted. He persisted in his pursuit of me, though. He bought me a plastic ring and he took a cigar band and placed it around his finger as a sign of our marriage to come.

I had on a pair of shorts with one side red and the other side white. In the past, Donald had made the comment to me, over and over, that I was built like a woman. On this particular day he said so often and with so much emotion in his voice that it sent chills up my spine. He acted like he could not take his eyes off of me. He kept smiling, smacking his lips, rubbing his hair down and staring at my shorts.

I had never reached the point where I was comfortable around him but by this time I was not afraid of him. The next day was the Fourth of July and I had on a red, white and blue striped halter top with the matching shorts and blue suede mandrill sandals with the leg ties that tied up to the knees. Donald was driving down the street as I walked to the corner store. He pulled his car over and called me to come to him. By the time I reached the car he was standing outside the door.

"You arousing me," he said with a very sexy smile. I didn't know exactly what arousing meant but the way he said the word and looked at me, I had a very good idea of what it was. "Where you going?"

"I'm going to the store and then over to Almaree's house."

"I came to take you to the park. It's the Fourth of July, don't you want to go to the park to be with me, baby?"

I looked in the car and saw Killzone, another friend of theirs, sitting in the back seat and said, "Me and Alma are going over to hang around at the swimming pool in Garfield."

Donald walked up close to me and put his arm around my waist, "I want you to be with me today," he said.

"You know I can't have no boyfriend, Donald." I said as I pulled away from him.

He took my hand and pulled me to him. Then he walked me around until my back was to his car. He stood in front of me, trapping me so I could not move. He put both of his hands on either side of me and leaned in until his body touched mine. I was scared and extremely uncomfortable but I was too afraid to say anything to him. The only thing I knew to do was to simply start looking down at my feet. I wanted to look up or away but I couldn't even turn my face because he had rigidly pressed his right cheek against my left cheek and he held a firm stance. I was afraid to move. I asked him to let me move away from the car but he refused.

"I am very patient but…" his voice trailed off. He looked me from head to toe and continued, "If you wear those shorts again, I'll have to rape you."

He was smiling the whole time he spoke so I didn't understand that rape was something bad. That was the first time I had ever heard the word so I had no idea of what it meant.

"What is that?"

"Wear those shorts again and I'll show you."

He kissed me on the cheek and licked the side of my face. I felt sick inside and I got an eerie feeling from his words. Most of the times he talked to me I got an eerie feeling so when he did release me, I brushed off his comments, wiped my face dry, continued on my way to the store and then to Alma's house.

Lester walked up behind me while I was in the store and pulled the ribbons out of my hair. I tried to get them back but I just didn't feel like fighting with him.

"What's wrong...ain't got no fight in you today?" he asked.

I shook my head and whispered, "No," then I walked away from him. I paid for the things I wanted and left out of the store.

Lester ran out behind me and asked, "Where's your boyfriend?"

I looked at him and said, "Where's Dwanna?"

He took both of my hands and with one of the most sincere looks I had ever seen him display, he said, "She ain't my girlfriend. She is just somebody that lets all of us get some. So, I get mine."

I laughed and walked away from him.

"What you laughing at and where you going? Home is that way," he said as he pointed in the direction of my house.

"I ain't going home. I'm going somewhere else."

"Where?" he demanded.

"I ain't got to tell you nothing," I said with a sadness that permeated my entire body and weakened my vocal strength.

Then I thought about what Donald said to me. I was going to ask Lester if he knew what the word 'rape' meant but I decided not to say anything for fear of having him joke about me being stupid or dumb later. Lester walked with me for part of the way. At first he picked at me and pushed me around to try to make me fight him back and then he stopped.

"Why you messing with that old guy?" he asked softly with disappointment in his voice.

I looked at him with surprise. I thought everybody knew I was not the one pursuing a relationship with Donald. In fact, I was trying very hard to push him away from me without enraging him. He was so much older than me I didn't know what to expect or how to get away from him. I thought everyone, especially Lester, knew that.

"I ain't messing with nobody," I said so softly I wasn't even sure of whether or not he heard me.

"You love him?" he asked.

"Love! That boy comes over to my house and sits on my porch. He follows me to the playground and stuff and sometimes he gives me rides home from school. But I like him better than I like you 'cause at least he don't keep fighting me every time I see him."

He looked at me and shook his head as if I just didn't understand then he turned abruptly and walked home.

The following year I wore the pair of shorts I had worn on the Fourth of July when Donald told me he was going to rape me. I had forgotten all about his threat. It was my thirteenth birthday. I had a new pair of shorts to wear on the next day, the Fourth of July, and that pair appropriately fit the occasion for celebrating my thirteenth birthday. I walked out of the house to whistling from across the street. Lester and his brother were sitting on their steps. His big brother always flattered me with whistles and kind words. I walked down to the end of Maplerow, headed for the store. A few steps before I turned the corner onto East 143rd Street Donald drove up. He had Matthew, Speed and another guy in the car with him. He called me over to the car.

He looked at me and said, "Happy birthday babycakes! You are a teenager, now. Feel any different."

"Nope." I smiled but I still couldn't look into his face so I shyly looked down at my feet. He lifted my face up and looked me squarely in the eyes.

"What did I tell you I was going to do if you wore those shorts again?"

I immediately got nervous because the smile he usually spoke with was not on his face and his soft, alluring manner was harsh and cold.

"I don't know," I said.

"Do you love me yet?" he asked.

I looked down at my feet and I could not look at him.

"Do you love me yet?" he demanded.

I couldn't answer him because I was too frightened to speak.

"What did I tell you I was going to do if you wore those shorts again?" he asked again.

"I don't know, Donald."

"Yeah, you know. Didn't I tell you I was going to rape you if you wore those shorts again," he asked.

"I don't know what that means," I whispered softly as I looked up at him through tear-filled eyes. Then my head dropped again and, again, I could only stare at my feet.

The men in the car were all shouting, "I want some too."

He lifted my face to make me look at him. "Listen, I want you to chose who you want to make love to you. If you choose me then I'll be very gentle with you and I'll still marry you when you grow up, but if you choose one of them then they gonna bust yo cherry wide open."

I tried to move away from him but he grabbed my arm and tightened the grip on it until it was unbearable.

"Please don't do this to me, Donald." I cried.

I screamed as loud as I could but I felt the cold steel of a sharp knife poke into my neck.

"Shut up," said one of the men in the car. He had rolled down the window and poked his knife into my neck. Donald took out a gun and pressed it into the small of my back.

"Get into the car," he insisted.

I started screaming and would not get in. I felt assured he would kill me if I got into that car and I doubted he would do anything to me on the street.

"Okay, don't get in, we'll walk you down the middle of your street and let the whole world see what we 'bout to do to you," said the guy in the back. "Oh yeah, and if you tell anybody about what we do to you, then we'll kill yo' mamma but we'll do the same thing to her first." he continued.

They walked me a few steps to the end of Maplerow and down the busiest street in the neighborhood, East 143rd Street. The neighborhood was still being developed and there were a lot of woods around. Donald told the guy I didn't know to drive his car down to Matthew's house and wait for them there. While he did that, they walked me down the middle of the street with a gun in my back and a knife to my neck. Several cars passed us but no one stopped to help me.

In the woods, they stripped all of my clothes off of me. I was standing there, naked and crying, while they tried to make me decide who I wanted. Donald was the smallest of all of the men and I believed he really would take it easy on me. He sat there with a hurt look on his face, as if I was hurting his feelings by not saying his name. Speed took the gun from Donald's hand and placed it at my temple.

"You betta open that damn mouth of yours and choose before I blow yo' brains out."

I screamed out, "Donald."

He jumped to his feet and ran over to me. He picked me up and carried me to a spot where they could not see us. I begged him to let me go. He promised he would not let them kill me and he would not let them hurt me. I continued to plead with him but to no avail. When he put me down, he took off his shirt and laid it on the ground. He picked me up again and laid me on his shirt. He kept kissing me and telling me how much he loved me...he loved me the first time he ever saw me. I kept twisting and turning my face away from him but he grabbed me by the chin and held it firm.

He ran his tongue all over my face and lips. I bit him as he kissed me but that made him kiss me harder. Every time he kissed me, he said, "Love at first sight, that's what it was with you. Love at first sight." He kissed my entire body and then he pushed himself into me. When my vulva tore, he cried. "I knew you were a virgin. I knew it. I am the first man to make love to you. Don't worry about what happens here today, I'm still going to marry you when you grow up. Cause' I was the first man to ever make love to you!" He looked at me tenderly with tears in his eyes. He played with my hair and kept kissing me. He brushed my hair down and said, "Don't worry about what happens here today. I'm going to marry you when you grow up. I was the first man to make love to you and to love you, fully. It was love at first sight with you. I was your first lover."

I spit on the ground and with a shaky, uncontrolled voice filled with hatred I screamed, "You did exactly what you said you were going to do...you raped me!"

The other two men got tired of waiting and they found where we were, one after the other both men raped me.

Lester heard about what was being done to me and he came to my rescue. He was only thirteen, himself. Matthew, Donald and Speed were twenty, twenty-one and twenty-three. By the time Lester reached me I was lying on the ground balled up in a knot and bleeding from them jumping up and down inside of me. Speed still had Donald's gun in his hand when Lester ran up to him. He cocked the gun and fired it in the air. That didn't stop Lester; he kept running toward them. He must have immobilized Speed. He hit him in the face so hard he fell to his knees. Lester took the gun from him and pointed it at the other two. They both had knives. They dropped their knives and ran. Lester took off his shirt and wrapped it around me. Then he picked me up and carried me all the way home.

I was obliged to Lester for saving me. I thought he would make fun of me for having something like that happen to me but he never did. Instead, he wanted to take care of me - to date me. He had always wanted to date me from the first time we met. He explained the reason we fought every day was so we could have contact with each other. I guess I always did know he liked me and in my heart of hearts, I liked him too. But his act of courage indebted me to him for what I thought was going to be the rest of my life.

I did feel safe with him and for the next twelve years I dated him and he controlled and dictated my life. And, even though Lester was there to protect me the day I was raped, he presented just as great a threat to my wellbeing later in life. We had become so close it somehow made sense to him that we should kill ourselves so we could be together forever. He tried to kill us by driving into a pole on E. 143rd Street. He was going about 120 miles an hour and had taken his hands off of the steering wheel. I grabbed the wheel and steered the car. It really must have been God guiding the car and taking care of that situation because within a few minutes the car ran out of gas and slowed to a complete stop a few yards away from the pole. Because of those experiences I had not felt safe around men another day in my life since my thirteenth birthday, and, I shuttered and trembled each time I had to walk down E. 143rd Street.

When I was about twenty-five years old I did meet a man who helped me get away from Lester. His name was Max. He also helped me plan the murder of the three men who raped me. He was very good to me and would have done anything for me...even murder. We had staked out the plot of land where they had raped me and had planned for the entire year to kill them on my twenty-sixth birthday. The thirteenth anniversary of my thirteenth birthday and the day I lost my spirit and will to live. Donald had spent time in a military prison and Speed and Matthew were in and out of State prison. Max insisted I become friends with them so they would trust me, go places with me and want to protect me from men like them. Being friends with them was the hardest thing I ever had to do in my life. But their insistence on communicating with me made it easier than I thought. Every time I saw one of them I envisioned them getting killed. Donald sent me letters, cards and rings in the mail all of the time. He was in and out of prison and each time he'd get out, he would go by my parents' house. He still asked me to marry him. In his mind, he never did anything wrong, he thought I would want him more after he 'made love to me.' He did regret having his two friends take part in our pre-marital get together.

I should have won an academy award because during that year I was planning their death. Anyone would have thought we were the best of friends. Anyone would have thought I was in love with Donald. I stayed sick the entire year while I planned their demise. I was sick in my spirit and sick in the head. But, I was going to kill them if it was the last thing I ever did in life. My plan was to have them meet me at an after-hours dance club on Euclid Avenue. Max would have two guys planted in the club and one in the alley. Max's friends would act like they were harassing me and I would make a scene and leave out the back door when I saw Donald and his friends entering the front door. Donald and his friends would, of course, follow me out into the alley. Max's two friends would act like they were trying to get me into their car.

The other one would knock them out as they walked through the door. They would tie and gag them and take them to the park and rape and kill them. I was going to be there making comments to them about how it felt to be loved by three men in the woods! I wanted the men to take turns on them, so that each one would have to live with the shame of being raped by three men!

Boy, that was really something...I had that planned out perfectly. Max's friends were huge and they had just gotten out of jail in Alabama. I had the shovels that would be used to dig their graves in the trunk of my car. I had even thought about having them dig their own graves after they were raped so they could go to their graves thinking they had taken part in their own murder...just like I thought for all of those years...if I had just NOT put on that particular pair of shorts that day, or if I hadn't been so flattered by the fact that Donald was cute and he liked me...maybe none of that would have ever happened to me. The nature of the beast in them was the kind that hurt little girls and people just because they wanted something from them...something nobody had a right to take! I wanted them to die for what they had done to me...I wanted them to die over and over. I wanted them to know I was the one responsible, but they too, were responsible for what was about to happen to them!

I thought about this over and over and I felt no remorse whatsoever. I felt vindicated, like justice was about to be done. I had the strangest experience just three days before all of this was to take place. I was driving home from work, deep in thought about what was about to take place and trying to adjust to the idea that I would be spending the rest of my life in jail, when a loud, booming voice on the radio shouted, "This is the Reverend R. W. Schambach of Tyler, Texas. I'm talking about forgiveness here today!" He went on to say, "If you cannot forgive others, then God will not forgive you. Regardless of what alts you hold against your fellow man, you have got to forgive him!"

I turned the channel because I didn't want to hear anything about forgiveness...not after living with that kind of shame, degradation and fear for thirteen years. I turned to a different channel and that booming voice shouted, "This is the Reverend R. W. Schambach...If you cannot forgive others, how can you expect God to forgive you? Someone may have hurt you really bad; they may have gone so far as to physically hurt you, rape you or maybe even caused the death of someone you love dearly."

"Yeah, they killed me thirteen years ago, they caused the death of my spirit, I am a walking corpse...I hate them and I want them to die. They can't be allowed to continue to do this to people.   I have to stop them...they have to die!"

I turned the channel again and that booming voice said, "You are hurting because you hate. What they did has been over but the hatred you are carrying inside is killing you.   You have got to forgive those who have trespassed against you. You have got to learn to let God fight your battles. You have got to forgive them if you want God to forgive you."

I cried as I drove home and I cursed and swore and swore and cursed. I pushed the button to turn the radio off but that booming voice still filled my car as I drove. He offered a prayer of forgiveness so I prayed along with Reverend Schambach to ask God to help me and to forgive me. In that very moment I felt like a ton of bricks had been lifted off of me.

Within the year, each of the three rapists had been killed violently in jail. Donald was thrown into some type of machine that cut him to shreds. Speed had his throat cut from one side of his neck to the other. I was told his head was cut off completely and Matthew was tied down into his bed and stabbed 143 times. I never had to lift a finger against them and as strange as this may sound, when I prayed that prayer with Reverend Schambach I did really forgave them. So, I knew God forgave me for planning to kill them. He certainly spared my life. I can only imagine what it would have been like trying to live my life in jail.

CHAPTER NINETEEN

In the dream, East 143rd Street was entirely empty. Any other time it would have been filled with activity and overflowing with people and cars all times of the day and night. In the dream, though, I was the only human to be seen and everywhere I looked there were packs of wolves, numbering into the thousands. As I walked down the street, packs of wolves came from behind buildings and backyards and began following me. I was frightened but too frightened to run. I searched my body to see if I had anything that I could use to protect myself against the wolves, or at least to keep them at bay. I walked slowly down the street and glared into the windows of the houses searching for even the slightest sign some human activity. The curtains and drapes in all of the houses were pulled back and I could see clearly inside of all of them. There were wolves in every room of every house. I looked at the houses that had balconies and there were packs of wolves on each balcony. Wolves were even perched on the tops of the roofs of every house.

As I approached my house I noticed my neighbor's house was completely destroyed. This was the neighbor who stopped her car and shook her head in disapproval at me. The one who decided 'those boys were just playing.' I didn't give it much thought at the time but in recalling the dream I realized her house and Matthew's house were the only two that were totally destroyed. Wolves covered every inch of their property. As I approached each property, the wolves stopped all activity. They watched me and fell in line to follow me as I walked home.

I walked slowly up the four steps and stood on my front porch. I opened the door and went inside. It was empty but the wolves pushed and forced the door opened. They didn't fill up all of the rooms in my house. They filled up the hallway that led to the front door. They were all over the porch, on the steps, in the front yard and they filled up every inch of space on the entire street. After a few minutes about a dozen other wolves entered the living room area. I was afraid to sit down and I didn't want to stay in the house. I wanted desperately to find other people. I had not seen any wolves until I reached

East 143rd Street so, in my mind; it stood to reason that if I could get past East 143rd Street I might find people. My mother and stepfather were at work. At least that's where I had hoped they'd be, and Toot stayed at school late for the small fry track and field practice.

As I moved toward the door and finally out of the house and down the street, the wolves opened a pathway for me. There was a clear pathway all the way down Maplerow back to East 143rd Street. My eyes searched each house, yard and garage I passed. Again, everywhere I looked there were wolves, hundreds, maybe even thousands of them. When I reached the corner of East 143rd Street I turned left and walked up to Caine Avenue. My Aunt Marie and Uncle Alex lived on the corner of East 143rd Street and Caine. She had a big German Sheppard named Smokey that was mean and vicious. I wondered if Smokey would have been able to survive the wolves or if he was so vicious he scared the wolves away, just as he did everything else. I looked down to the end of the block because before I had rounded that corner, there were people. But this time wolves were coming together from both sides of the block and they were coming out of the houses along Caine in my direction.

I was hoping and even praying out loud that Smokey would have been in his doghouse. Whether or not he would have served any purpose or would have been able to fight off even one wolf was another story. I guess at that time I just wanted to see someone or even anything familiar. Smokey was a mean spirited dog. Having him around might have meant a quicker demise for me but the ferocious looks in the eyes of the wolves made me more fearful for my life than I had ever been with Smokey.

Every time I walked past Smokey he tried to attack me. He would run at me until his thick chain was stretched tight and pulled so hard it choked him. Still, he would try to get to me, he would be on his hind legs choking himself, growling and barking at me. I looked over to the corner of the house where Smokey would normally be but he wasn't there. I walked past his doghouse and looked inside and he was not there either.

Then it struck me. There weren't any other animals or people around, just me and the wolves.

I moved slowly toward the porch, peering into each window as I neared the front door. After a few seconds I realized I didn't see any wolves in the house so I ran quickly up the front steps and banged on the door. No one answered the door. I turned the doorknob and the door opened. I peeked inside of the house but I still didn't see any people or any wolves. I walked inside and ran up to the second floor. I opened the door and slowly walked in. I called out, in a small, scared voice for my Aunt Marie, my cousin Johnny, and my cousin Donna but no one answered. I was greeted by packs of huge black wolves with whitish-gray whiskers around their mouths. I didn't know what to do, but I did know I should not run. I also realized there was no one to call on for help.

Thinking I had no options, I decided to jump off of the balcony to kill myself. There, on the balcony, sat the largest albino wolf I had ever seen. Its head was almost up to my shoulders and its body was waist-high and about four and a half feet long. Without any more fear I walked passed the wolf and stepped up onto the banister of the balcony. I rationalized it would be less painful to kill myself than to be eaten alive by wolves. I stretched my arms out wide, closed my eyes and let myself fall forward. I felt the wind blow through my hair as I began to fall. Air filled my mouth and nostrils as I was forcefully and quickly pulled back onto the porch by the large wolf. I lay on the balcony floor looking up at the large wolf. He pulled me to my feet by the tail of my blouse and turned his head as though he was directing me to start walking. He nudged and pushed me out of the house past the other wolves. As I moved closer to the packs of wolves they moved aside and made a path for me to walk through. I walked out of the house and down the street. As I walked the wolves filed out of the houses and walked behind me. The big wolf or the alpha male walked in front of me. I walked back to my house and went inside. The large wolf and a few others came inside with me while the rest stayed outside. That's when I woke up.

I remember thinking the wolves had eminent domain, they had taken over the community and there was no one to oppose them. I looked at Anaghia as she shape shifted into the large alpha wolf that pushed and guided me out of the house. In the next second, Anaghia, the beautiful Native American Indian woman was again sitting next to me.

"It was you?" I gasped.

"Yes. I have been with you for a very long time."

CHAPTER TWENTY

"Have you never realized that you walked among us? That you walked up front directly behind me, the alpha wolf? Do you now realize we were here first, not the people of the street. We are restoring the spirit of our people and reclaiming our place in this world. Do you now realize you are not alone?"

I felt very secure and comfortable with her and what she had just said made perfectly good sense to me.

"Why now?"

"Because you need it now. Your spirit is in danger and your plea reached the Roll Call of the Dead a long time ago. But now, you are ready to accept your destiny and recapture your spirit. It is now the spirit world that responds to you. You have a foe gathering allies to work against you to do you great harm. The danger does not, however, lie with the foe, it lies in your actions...you had given up...you chose to die instead of fight. You must fight! You must regain your confidence and courage. You can defeat your enemies. Come with me, learn your ancestry and fight for your future."

In the next minute, Anaghia and I were walking across a huge grassy plain bound on two sides by a tremendous igneous rock mountain where streams of water flowed from the tops of the mountain down into rippling, brooks and lakes. There were woods where trees grew up to a hundred feet tall and lived for hundreds of years.

Immediately, I noticed there was something different about the air. It was fresh...very fresh and clean. It had not yet been polluted. There were Indian teepees scattered throughout the largest expanse of the plain. The teepees were flanked on three sides by thick, dense woods and the beautiful blue-gray mountains. Children were playing and horses, bears, wolves and other animals roamed freely among them. The horses appeared to be wild and none of the other animals or wolves were vicious. We went inside of one of the teepees. It was about thirty feet by thirty feet. It was much bigger than what I had expected. There were animal-skinned rugs on the floor and covering the bed.

An elder of the tribe was sitting in the center of the floor. He was a big man, tall in stature but thinly built. His hair was white and his skin was a burnt, brownish-tan and leather-like. He held a long thin tube with a cone-like bulb at the end of it. It was opened at the end and he used it like a pipe. His eyes twinkled and crinkled as he looked at me and smiled. He rocked back and forth and stared at me as though I should have recognized him. He sat there and went into a trance-like state. In the second he closed his eyes I was back in the woods, laying on the grass watching the shadows and the shadow of a tall, thin stranger moving toward me. A few minutes later he opened his eyes and looked at me, again.

I wanted to scream and run out of the teepee. I did recognize him! He was the man in the woods. The man I devoured, the man I thought was there to harm me. I thought for a minute I was being brought to him so he could exact his revenge. But somehow that just didn't make sense. I doubted whether it was the man at all. I kept asking myself why I had been brought to a man I devoured in my dream. Finally, I resolved it be I had made a mistake, that that was not the man at all. Anaghia knew my thoughts. She squeezed my hand and said, "Yes, it is he! But it is you who do not understand."

I couldn't answer. I was consumed with thoughts that I was about to be ambushed, but why? And, where on earth was this place? Or, was it on earth at all? These and more questions raced through my mind. The man in the center of the room stood up. He was very tall and ominous looking. Being in his presence made me nervous and afraid. He sat his pipe-like tube down and walked over to me. He reached out his arms as though he wanted me to walk into his embrace and hug him after what had happened in the woods. He smiled but shook his head, "No."

"No. Now what? I don't know what you want from me," I cried.

I could feel Anaghia's grip tighten on my hand. She walked over to the man and hugged him. As her arm wrapped around the round of his back, her body moved right through his as if he was invisible or not there.

I cried out, "What on earth is going on, here? What has all of this got to do with me?"

He reached out his arms again for me to embrace him. My fear began to dissipate. I still didn't want to go to him but I was being drawn into him. I moved, not by my will, but by his will toward him. I looked back at Anaghia as I continually moved forward. My eyes, heart and thoughts pleaded with her to pull me back. When I turned back to look at the man he grabbed my hand and pulled me closer. My body passed right through his. I felt bursts of energy exploding from the top of my head down to the tips of my toes. The energy was hot and it burned in a very peculiar way. It felt like ice burning me from the inside out. I looked down as we stood inside of each other and I could see a million atoms circling each other. Our bodies cast a bright light throughout the teepee that would have blinded a normal human being but it didn't blind either of us. The light stretched out in a million directions. An explosion of colors burst through us. The colors were brilliant and they went from white to yellow to red to orange to blue and then to black. After our energies mixed, I moved through on to the other side of him. For another few minutes we remained as hot as fire and had ceased to be in human form...we had become energy, pure energy. The feeling was indescribable. In those few minutes that our energies mixed I gained the strength and the wisdom of the elders that went before me. I realized this man was in the woods to ignite my strength and diminish my fear. I had to devour him in order to have all of the other experiences that were to come. He was there to make me defend myself, to teach me I had the power and courage to devour instead of giving in without a fight to survive. It was then I knew I had to swallow him to get the spirits that were waiting to protect me, inside of me.

I experienced several lifetimes. In one moment I saw a beautiful Indian woman, Mytanna, leaning over a stream of fresh lake water bathing her baby, Anagh. A family, the Washingtons, rode up in a covered wagon. They had somehow gotten separated from their wagon train. The woman could barely move but she forced herself to get out to speak to Mytanna.   Mytanna was not afraid of them but she was curious about the couple because they looked so different from her and her people. It was the first time she had ever seen blue eyes, blonde hair and pale-colored skin on a person. Neither could speak the other's language so they had a hard time communicating. Mrs. Washington placed her hand on her stomach and the other on the wood plank that ran across the wagon. Her legs buckled but she steadied herself by holding onto the wagon.   Mytanna could see Mrs. Washington was pregnant and very soon she would be giving birth. Her large round stomach hung low which meant she was carrying a boy child. Boys had a tendency to come early and to punch and kick a lot right before their arms are pinned down in the birth canal. Mytanna knew Mrs. Washington was in a lot of pain and if she gave birth in that wagon she would bleed to death judging by the size of her stomach. Mrs. Washington was a small-framed woman. The only weight she had gained was sitting in the center of her stomach. His large stomach sat on her body like a watermelon sitting on a thin branch and it was weighing her down. It looked like her back would break if she didn't give birth soon. That was a big baby and it was moving into position to come out of her. Mytanna put Anagh on her back and filled her leather pouch with water. She motioned for the Washingtons to get water also. They filled their jars and pots and followed Mytanna back to her reservation.

All of the people on the reservation came out of their teepees and followed the wagon to Mytanna's teepee. She took Mrs. Washington into her teepee while Mr. Washington sat nervously in the back of the wagon. Mytanna knew a traditional squat and push birth was out of the question for Mrs. Washington. She could tell the baby had moved into an awkward position judging by the bulges on both sides of Mrs. Washington's stomach.

She gently laid Mrs. Washington on the bed of grass and leaves covered by animal skins. Mrs. Washington's labor became more intense. She screamed out in pain and Mr. Washington rushed in to sit at her side. Mytanna rinsed her hands and covered them with some brown dried leaves she took out of a pouch that sat in the corner of her teepee. She took two large wooden posts and stuck them into the ground on both sides of Mrs. Washington. She took two leather straps and tied Mrs. Washington's hands to the posts. Mr. Washington didn't like the idea of his wife's hands being tied down. He snatched one of the leather straps up and shook his head to indicate his disagreement to Mytanna's impending actions. Mytanna snatched the strap from his hand and tied Mrs. Washington's hand back to the post.

Mr. Washington said, "No, I will not have you tie her hands," and he untied her hand.

Mytanna began to help Mrs. Washington off of the bed and she motioned for them to leave. Just as Mrs. Washington looked at her husband another pain hit her. The pains were getting closer and closer and she fell to her knees.

She cried out as she sat on the floor, "Please, you just go back to the wagon if you can't stand to see this. This baby is coming. I don't care what she does to my hands. This baby is about to come and this woman has obviously delivered babies before. She would not have all of this stuff in here if she didn't do this type of thing often. So, what's it going to be? Are you going to go or stay?"

Mr. Washington hung his head down and walked out of the teepee.

Mytanna crushed the leaves and mixed it with small amounts of dark red dirt she poured out of another pouch. She put a small amount of the mixture into Mrs. Washington's mouth and fed her a small amount of water. Next she took a small bowl and poured water into it. She dipped her hands into the water until it was murky and filled with the brown leaves. She spread the murky mixture up and down her arms and over her hands. First Mytanna pushed three fingers into Mrs. Washington to see how much Mrs. Washington had dilated. Her three fingers easily entered Mrs. Washington. She stood back and looked up the birth canal to see if she could see the baby and tell how far it was up the canal. The mixture Mytanna put on her hands would numb Mrs. Washington and lessen the pain as Mytanna opened the path for the baby to come out. She covered her hands and arms with the substance up to her elbows. She made a fist and stuck it far up into Mrs. Washington. Once she was far enough inside to feel the baby, she turned him so that he would come out without problems. Then she began twisting her arm from left to right, relaxing and opening her hand and expanding her fingers as she slowly withdrew her arm. In the next two minutes, a baby boy was sliding out of Mrs. Washington. Immediately following the baby came the sack that held him for nine months. Mytanna took the baby and placed it on the bed next to Mrs. Washington. Next she placed a flat, round rock on the bed between the baby and the sack. She stretched the cord across the rock and in one swift movement she sliced the cord in half. She took a small brown reef and lit it with the fire that burned in the middle of the teepee. She burned the end of the cord that was connected to the baby's naval.

Mytanna rinsed her hands and arms and took three large purple wild berries and placed them in Mrs. Washington's mouth. She chewed the berries and within minutes she began to feel relaxed and comfortable. Mytanna pulled Mrs. Washington's dress up above her waist and poured the remainder of the murky water over her genitalia. Then she mixed a pot of hot boiling water with a pot of cold water until it was warm to touch. She stood over Mrs. Washington and held the pot so it released a steady stream of the warm water until all of the blood was cleaned away. Mytanna took a blanket, tore it into quarters and wrapped one quarter of it around Mrs. Washington and another around her baby. Next, she went to the wagon to get Mr. Washington to take him to his wife and new baby. As soon as she appeared at the door he jumped out of the wagon and ran in to see about his wife, shoving Mytanna out of his way as he passed her. Mr. Washington didn't trust Mytanna to deliver his child. He thought of her as savage and unclean but he had no other options to provide for the safe delivery of his child so he allowed Mytanna to take over.

CHAPTER TWENTY-ONE

In the next minute I was looking through Mytanna's eyes and could see and hear the screams and cries of the Chewani tribe being slaughtered. Droves of covered wagons and men riding on the backs of horses with long sticks that were tipped with fire were setting teepees on fire while elders, men, women and children were still inside. Men in covered wagons tore down teepees and trampled over them. I saw women and children being run down and trampled over by the men on horses and the wheels of the covered wagons rolling over old men who could not get out of their way. I heard gunshots ring out over the cries of her people, the Chewani people...somehow these were now my people! And I saw men with guns, going from teepee to teepee killing everyone inside, taking food, water, silver, animal skins. Mytanna ran frantically from the front opening of the teepee to the back. There was no way out except to run into the hands of those murderous men. She looked to Mr. and Mrs. Washington for help. Mr. Washington hung his head down and Mrs. Washington turned her head away. She quickly realized the Washingtons were not in position to help anyone. She grabbed the sharp rock she used to cut the cord for Mrs. Washington's baby. She tied a soft cloth around Anagh's mouth to muzzle any sounds he may have made and escaped out the back of the teepee by cutting down the back seam of the teepee. Mrs. Washington positioned herself in front of the hole so no one would suspect how Mytanna escaped. Mytanna heard the voices of men filling up the teepee as she fled deep into the woods. An old albino wolf she had nourished back to health stood in the center of the woods and watched her. He led her and Anagh away from the fallen reservation and deep into the woods.

Mytanna and Anagh lived with the wild animals for several months. There was no indication anyone else from her tribe had survived the slaughter. She searched the woods for food and signs that another Chewani had been there. Each day she was able to find food for Anagh and herself but she found no evidence of any other Chewani people in the area. She marked the trees with small symbols. These symbols were used by the scribes of the tribe and were only recognizable to the Chewani people. To the naked eye the symbols looked like natural markings or scratches made by wild animals. Her hope was if, by chance, there was some other Chewani alive they could work together to take revenge on the people in the wagon train.

Each day Mytanna lived with the memory that all of her people were dead because she had brought the enemy into their reservation. She didn't know such devastation would result from her one act of kindness. Perhaps the same thing would have happened even if she had not taken the Washingtons to her home.

While on the mountaintop, Mytanna dipped and washed herself in the cool stream of water that flowed off of the rocks. The men who destroyed the reservation had settled and made camp. They had built houses and hunted the animals in the woods where Mytanna lived. One of the men saw Mytanna atop the mountain. He made his way up the mountain with the thought of raping and killing her. This man watched Mytanna as she went back to the place where she was living. Day after day, for seven days straight, he watched her as she bathed herself and her son. Mytanna's hearing was keen and exact. She heard the footsteps of the man as he walked nearer to her but she would not turn to face him. As the man moved closer the birds in the trees screamed out warnings for Mytanna but she didn't run. She was looking at her destiny. She was connected to the spirits of the dead and she knew she, too, had to die.

In her vision, she saw Anagh being raised by the wolves and growing into a man. She saw him in a new place with a wife, whose hue was even darker than those of the Chewani people. She saw Anagh and his wife happy with children so she knew he would be all right. She knew the man didn't care about Anagh. She could feel the thoughts of the man as he approached her. He thought the wolves would kill Anagh or he would simply starve to death after he killed Mytanna. She knew the man walked behind her but still she walked, naked, to the center of the grassy plain. She walked tall and slow as the man from the caravan of covered wagons sneaked up behind her. She looked at the ground and examined his shadow behind hers. It was long and tall and it grew shorter as he came nearer to her. She felt his thoughts as he reached out to place his large hand around her mouth and to choke her with the other hand.

The second before he touched her, Mytanna prayed to the Holy Spirit to take her. Her spirit left her body and went deep into the earth and mixed with the essence of the spirits of her dead ancestors, energy of the heavens was cast to the ground and blended into the spiritual mix. Before the man could touch her, her name had been added to the Roll Call of the Dead. Her body was still warm, hot in fact, when the man grabbed her from behind. Thinking she was alive he pinned both of her hands together in a vice-like grip with his large hands and threw her to the ground. He never gave it a thought that she didn't move because he was busy raping her and trying to tear her insides apart. When he finished he immediately broke her neck. Breaking her neck served two purposes for the man. First, despite their communication gap, she would never be able to tell anyone about his brutality and she would not recognize him from the time she delivered his baby boy to his wife.

Her naked body lay awkwardly on the ground. Her neck had been broken and her body was curled almost in the shape of a nine with her head touching her knees. The man took note of the awkward position her body was in but he quickly dismissed it and walked away. He glanced back at her body one last time and stopped abruptly in his tracks when he noticed her body was now completely curled into a circle. Even though the blades of grass were tall enough to cover her, he could still see her body had shifted positions. The spirits moved underneath the earth where her body lay and from the heavens above. I watched as her body transformed from a beautiful woman into a large snake. I watched the snake as it slithered up behind the man and devoured him. Then I watched the snake move through the grassy plain so quickly I could barely tell it from cracks in the earth. I watched the hundreds and hundreds of wolves emerge from the woods and the snake stop moving when it reached the wolf pack. I saw the snake transform into a wolf and lead them back to the Chewani reservation where the settlers had taken over their land. My heart filled with pride and sympathy for the innocent ones as the wolves devoured every single person in the camp leaving nothing but the wooden structures standing.

The realization hit me that the spot where Mytanna died and was restored was the same spot where my dream began. I, too, lay there naked, almost hidden by the long green blades of grass. In the next second, I was watching Donald as he laid his shirt on the ground. Everything that happened was familiar. The place I was raped is the place where Mytanna was raped and her spirit left her body. It was the place I awoke to in my dream. Of course, there are houses and roads in that place today but I knew it was the same place. In the moment that he laid me down and began to rape me, I gave up on life and my spirit also left my body.

When Mytanna's spirit left her body, the essence of her life first went into a snake who killed the man who brought harm to her and her people and it leapt into the wolves that lay in wait, deep in the woods, as did the spirits of all those who had been killed in the attack months earlier. When my spirit left my body I thought it went into a deep void. I wanted to die I didn't know how to fight.   My enemy and the weakness of my mind enslaved me. Even though my spirit moved into the snake and then into the wolf and there was no one left to harm me, I didn't call out to the Holy Spirit that was waiting to save me.   I didn't acknowledge the victory.   I gave in to the defeat of being raped and tormented. I didn't want to fight. I wanted to die. I didn't know how to fight such an enemy.   The wolves raised Anagh and took revenge on those who destroyed their people and land, killing everyone responsible for the death of the Chewani people. I could only surmise that my spirit laid in wait until I could understand the significance of the dream.

CHAPTER TWENTY-TWO

I experienced several different lives and cultures during those ensuring seconds. I came to understand the role of the wolves in my life. One of the lives I experienced was my great, great, grandmother who was a Chewani descendant of Mytanna. I could see Anaghia in several settings of the people I had met during my voyager experience. I saw a person who resembled me strongly several times, too. During my journey the energies and the life forces of my ancestors filled me and burned inside of me like fire from the top of my head to the bottom of my feet. With every experience the energies seemed to be settling inside of me and strengthen me. The hot, fiery heat that saturated my body began to dissipate. It felt like someone was blowing cool air on me. It started at the top of my head and moved down to the tip of my toes. My heart was heavy and filled with grief. I wanted to cry but I could not utter a sound. I looked up at Anaghia and said, "I am beginning to see, but I still do not understand."

She nodded and said, "You are not alone and you will survive. There are many great things in store for you. You are destined to change the future for many people. You must not allow yourself to be destroyed by others and you are not permitted to destroy yourself. You had to face the image of destruction that loomed large over you. You had to devour the strong adversary that immobilized and crippled you. You had to taste the blood of the enemy. You had to defeat your fears. You had to face, devour and taste the blood of man. Now you are free, unrestricted by conformance, fear, and doubt. You are free to move on to your destiny!"

I buried my face in my hands and cried. Before that day I had never really reconciled with the thought that I wanted to die but I didn't have the courage to kill myself. Ever since I was raped I wanted to die to escape the shame and disgrace I suffered. I wanted to stop being afraid of every man who said he loved me only to find out later he wanted to hurt me or kill me. I wanted to stop watching every person who watched me and stop looking around every corner for someone to jump out and hurt me. I wanted to wear shorts and have fun and stop wearing the long pants and unflattering clothes. Every day of my life I expected someone to hurt me, every day of my life I dreaded hearing the words I want to marry you, and every year I dreaded the thought of facing my birthday and the awful surprises it held for me.

I never told anyone what had happened to me and I lived in fear it would happen again every day since then. I was among the living dead trying to get to my burial grounds. Dying would have been a relief. Afraid to experience life to its fullest degree in fear someone would know I was weak and vulnerable; and, the very essence of my soul was raped and taken away from me, was a daily cross to bear. Being attractive to men was not an advantage or a good thing; it was a curse that could culminate into my demise. I couldn't do anything that would bring attention to me without putting myself deep into the background.

Everything good I did was for the sake of others and I surrounded myself with women who I thought was much prettier than me so I would be able to fit, easily, into the background. I didn't feel like I deserved anything good to happen to me. In the dark silence that loomed in my mind, I had to admit that I was, at times, attracted to Donald. I liked the idea that he thought he was in love with me. Even though Donald made me feel extremely uncomfortable most of the time, the fact that he paid so much attention to me made me feel special, like I was a grown-up. But, in essence, I was a foolish child who should have avoided him like the plague, just like my parents told me to do. I felt like I was partially responsible for what had happened and because of that I ended up feeling like nothing more than damaged goods. Not being a virgin took away everything I thought love was about. Giving of yourself to one person who would love you for the rest of your life. Never knowing another man in that way. Without being a virgin, I had nothing. I was nothing. Not only was my virginity taken from me but my mind and my peace of mind was taken from me.

I was paranoid, suspicious, untrusting and jealous of everybody in the world who could live a normal life. Because of that I never let anyone get too close to me. I never dug too deep into anyone else in fear that the shallow, frightened, little girl that lived deep inside of me would be uncovered and hurt in the process. Over time, I became reclusive and out-of-touch to the point of not knowing how to connect to people. I began to feel like an alien who spoke and looked like everyone else but who would shrivel up and die if anyone else's emotions touched me.

I lived a lonely, unhappy, unfulfilled life even though it appeared that I had everything. I had everything but peace of mind and the knowledge of true love. I didn't trust love and I didn't know love. I am sure old boyfriends have loved me dearly and maybe even Jerry but I never let myself experience it. The best thing I could do for myself was to put on a good and strong front to keep from ever being raped again.

I kept looking for the hammer to drop on the top of my head or the hand to grab my neck and take out the knife to slit my throat. I challenged love and pushed it away, as far away as I could push it. I often questioned why I stayed with Jerry so long without really loving him. Not loving him or any other man was safe for me. I didn't think he loved me and it really didn't matter to me. I was haunted by my loneliness even though I never had a chance to be alone. Every night I lay in the bed looking at the ceiling, wondering what it must feel like to love someone, other than my parents, siblings and good friends. I wanted to know love from one special man but I feared it and I didn't trust it, so I resolved to live without it.

My brothers and sisters were all out of town and my mother and stepfather were now deceased. The closest person to me was my friend, Aleena; she was like a sister to me. I love Aleena and the models like I love my brothers and sisters. We have a very strong bond that will never break. But I kept others far away from me. I never let too many people into my life as friends because I love my friends and I have to trust my friends and I didn't trust too many people. I knew I had all of their love and respect and I love and respect all of them.

Most days I cried when I was alone because it hurt, deep in my heart, to acknowledge and accept the fact I would never know what it felt like to love a man, to cleave to a husband and forsake the rest, or enjoy the intimate love that takes place between a man and a woman when their souls blend in perfect harmony. I accepted the fact I would never have a soul mate with whom I could exchange love for love.

I longed for family and through this voyager experience I learned that throughout the history of my family, my loved ones had been destroyed at the hands of outsiders posing to be lovers and friends. It was time to end the destruction. It was time to survive the devastation of the outsiders. I knew then that Jerry was an outsider and, knowingly or not, he was the catalyst for the cycle of destruction to begin again.

In that moment I no longer feared living and I no longer invited death. I knew that the spirits of my ancestors were with me and I was not alone. Whatever weaknesses were in me were gone and I was ready to survive. I lifted my head, renewed in spirit and strong in my conviction to survive. I welcomed all challengers to my survival and I embraced the powerful force within me that made me know my role in life was to be a conqueror.

Just then the doorknob rattled and Jerry walked into the apartment. The door to my bedroom was still closed but in my mind I could see what took place between Jerry and Blascey at the restaurant before he left to come home. He was strangely calm, almost as though he had been sedated. I sensed his confusion. I saw an image of Blascey squeezing an eyedropper and releasing a drop of a very light bluish-green liquid in Jerry's cup while he was in the restroom. I saw him returning to his seat.

I heard him say, "I am in love ..."

Blascey cut him off at that point by putting her finger up to his lips. She stuck her finger inside of his mouth and rubbed it across his gums.

"Hold that thought but have your drink first."

I could see the pupils in his eyes expand as he moved her hand away from his lips.

"Okay, I think I need a drink."

He took the exquisitely crafted flute and drank all of the Cold Duck champagne, including the bluish-green liquid, in one big gulp. Then he sat back and stared at

Blascey. She sat back and watched him for a few minutes and then she put a drop of the liquid in her glass and drank it. Her pupils enlarged after about a second. She placed her finger in her mouth and started rubbing her gums. In seconds they both were laughing even though neither one had said anything. It was then I realized Blascey was actually drugging Jerry. I didn't know what he was going to say and I couldn't feel his emotions at the time. Within minutes Andrew and Lillian walked into the restaurant and sat next to Blascey and Jerry. Blascey asked them if they were ready.

Lillian slammed her fist against the table and screamed, "No!"

Blascey lost her temper and said, "Look, you lunatic, you are going to do whatever I say or else you will find yourself back in Fair Hill." Then she looked at Andrew and said, "Now what the hell you got to say?"

Andrew looked at Blascey and said, "Didn't you say she turned into some kind of animal and did that to your face?"

Blascey nodded her head, "Yes."

He moved close to her face and screamed, "Well then I ain't got nothing to say 'cause I ain't got nothing to do with this mess. I ain't gonna have her turn into no animal and do that to me."

Andrew and Lillian got up to walk away but then Lillian turned around and walked back to the table. Lillian has a second hatpin that she was supposed to use on me after Jerry stuck me with him. Hers was simply a backup, but Blascey told her to use it on me regardless of my condition. Lillian took the hatpin out of her purse and asked, "What's on this pin?"

Blascey rolled her eyes at Lillian and said in a very demeaning voice, "Nothing. It's just something that will make her dizzy for a while and yours is just in case there's not enough solution on Jerry's."

"It ain't nothing in there that will kill her?" Lillian and Andrew both asked, in unison.

"No, I told you, it will make her dizzy," Blascey relented.

Lillian said, "You must really think we are crazy," then she jabbed the hatpin into Blascey's hand and ran out the door.

Blascey stood up and screamed out in the loudest voice possible, "Somebody, get me to the hospital, and be quick about it!" then she dropped to the floor.

The bedroom door swung open and Jerry stood in the center of the doorway. He looked at me as though he dared me to try to escape. He moved his head forward to focus his eyes on the bed then he shook his head as though he was clearing an absurd thought from his mind.

"What is that?" he asked.

I looked at him but didn't answer.

"Did I see something on the bed next to you?" he asked softly.

"I don't know. What did it look like?"

He shook his head and stumbled back a few feet. "I thought I saw something on the bed. I just don't know what the heck it was," he said in a low, frightened voice.

"Jerry, relax. There is nothing on the bed. I looked out the window and Anaghia had transformed into the beautiful nighthawk. She was perched on the banister. Jerry looked at me and then out the window.

"Look at that big bird on the banister. I don't think I've ever seen anything like that before." He walked over to the bed and sat next to me.

"Something strange has been going on."

I shook my head and whispered, "Yes."

"I can't put my finger on it. Can you?" He asked as he searched my face for telltale signs of what was going on.

I sat there without answering him. I was broken-hearted because I realized so much of our problem was my fault. Jerry was reacting badly to it...trying to kill me and all...but so much of our problems stemmed from my inability to love him so, it really was my fault. I was always too afraid to be a wife to him or anyone. And now, I was right back on my aunt's porch about to jump off of the banister and being pulled to safety by the wolf. It was time for me to walk with the wolf with understanding and acceptance and to stop running from life, my life! I wanted to cry because of the damage I had done over the years. Jerry had a sweet, sad look on his face and the warmth in his heart reached out and surrounded me. It felt as though I have been enveloped in a warm, soft, fluffy cloud. I knew then he actually did love me but that in his weakness he was willing to allow someone to manipulate him into destroying me. He looked at me and tears welled up in his eyes. I looked away. I got up and walked into the living room.

Jerry followed me into the living room and sat next to me on the sofa. He took my hand in his. I didn't feel threatened so I didn't resist. He was sincere and in genuine pain when he said he didn't want our marriage to end. I knew one thing and that was ... even though I had been with him all of those years I didn't love him and it was time to stop causing so much pain for each of us. I had to leave. He reached over to hug me and I let him.

"It was love at first sight for me."

I pulled away from him because I wanted to explain things to him. He misinterpreted my intentions and immediately got angry when I pulled away. He jumped to his feet and put his hand in his pocket. I could see he was toying with the idea of jabbing me with the hatpin. I didn't want to scare him and I wasn't afraid of him so I asked, "Do you really want to see me dead, Jerry?"

He shook his head, "No," and turned to walk out the door. He put his hand on the doorknob and cracked the door open. He looked around at me and turned, again, ready to leave. I transported in front of the door before he could get out. Instantly, he dropped to the ground. He had fainted.

I lifted him onto the sofa and turned on the television. The eleven o'clock news was reporting a story about Thomas. Thomas was in a strait jacket in the back of an ambulance. He had gone back to the university and drove his car into the security guard's station. He refused to get out of the car so the security guard called the police on him. By the time they arrived he was crawling from the front seat of his car to the back seat, afraid to allow anyone to touch him. He claimed he couldn't be sure they were not people who turned into wolves. Poor Thomas, why didn't you just leave well enough alone? None of this would have ever happened to you. Right before I got ready to turn the television off, Thomas let out a big howl.

"She's a werewolf," he said and he let out another big howl.

"No," I said softly, "not a werewolf, Thomas...a wolf, just a plain ole' wolf, trying to survive the outsiders!"

Thomas looked around the car as though he was trying to figure out where the voice he heard had just come from. Again, I said in a soft whisper, "Sometimes you just have to let well enough alone, Thomas. The next time you see a wolf, get out of his way...don't try to fight it because there is no win for you. Be safe Thomas, be safe."

Thomas was paralyzed with fear. He climbed back into the front seat of his called, and lay balled up and whimpering like a child who had been left in a dark room...a child who was afraid to open his eyes to see what dark possibilities lay in wait for him.

Jerry finally woke up. He sat straight up on the sofa and grabbed my arm. He rubbed it and touched it to make sure I was all in one piece. His hands were trembling. He looked at me with tears in his eyes.

"I think I'm going crazy," he cried softly.

"No, you're not going crazy."

He sat back and stared at me without saying a word.

"I need to say something to you and I'm not quite sure of how I should say it without you thinking I'm crazy," I said softly.

"Go ahead. Maybe what you have to say will clear up what I think I saw in the bedroom and at the door a few minutes ago," he answered.

I knew it would clear it up for him but I wasn't ready to tell him that much of the story. I admitted many of the problems in our marriage were my fault. I told him I had not been happy any time during the seven and a half years we were married. He agreed he wasn't happy either at that point but he thought we could pull our marriage together. I knew we didn't have a marriage and never would. I was hiding out in our marriage, afraid to find and experience real and true love. I could not continue to live the lie.

I cried as I spoke because I was experiencing and releasing the pain of all of my ancestors who had been betrayed by their willingness to sacrifice their happiness to keep others happy and the devastation experienced by those who helped others when it proved to be dangerous for them. Their pain, as well as mine, was taking over my body. I was feeling the hands around the throat of Mytanna, the gunshots exploding in the bodies of my fleeing ancestors, the fire burning the flesh of my great, great, great grandfather, the pounding of the three men who raped me, and seeing the eyes of my neighbor glaring gleefully in the mirror in anticipation that I would be hurt badly or killed.

I knew I had to get away from Jerry. I felt terrible about the way I was making him feel. Any other time, I would have surrendered to his wishes and stayed in the marriage. I had changed. I was not weak and succumbing, I was strong and forbidding and for the first time in my life I felt entitled to live the way I saw fit.

Jerry took the needle out of his pocket and the vial of poison and laid it on the table. He looked at me and cried. He wanted to tell me more but I put my finger against his lips so he would not speak. I held him like a baby and rocked him until his eyes were closed from sleep. I sat there rocking him for more than two hours. Finally, without any interruptions he woke up. He got up to leave. He looked nervous and scared. He was hesitant to speak. After a few minutes, he smiled and asked, "So where do we go from here?"

I smiled genuinely and said, "Anywhere we want to go."

He kissed me for the last time and walked to the door. He looked at me and said, "The best moments of my life were spent loving you."

I watched him walk out the door and out of my life.

I woke up the next morning packing my bags. During the night I had a dream that I had moved to Atlanta, Georgia. Before my eyes were fully opened, I heard my voice saying in a joyful tone, "Why not?"

I looked around the room and thought about the things we had accumulated together and I knew I didn't want to take any of those things with me. I packed two suitcases and even though I didn't know where in Atlanta I would land, I knew I would land on my feet. I knew everything would be okay. The phone rang and it was my mechanic telling me that my car was ready and he would deliver it to my apartment in about ten minutes.

"Couldn't have been ready at a more opportune time," I said then I hung up the phone. "Ding dong the witch is dead." I sang out in a loud, happy voice. "The wicked witch is dead! Yeah!" I shouted in the loudest possible voice I could muster.

After I had everything I wanted, I stopped and looked around the room. Even though I didn't want to leave Aleena, I was ready to leave Cleveland. I walked toward the door and the phone rang again. It was Aleena. I had been trying to get in touch with her over the past month but could never catch up with her. I was busting open at the seams to tell her about my exploits of the past few days. I was going to break the news I'd be moving to Atlanta to her gently and at the right moment. We were so close it would be hard to tell her.

"Where on earth are you?" I asked.

"I'm calling to give you my phone number. I moved to Atlanta last month and I've been busy getting settled in here. It has been a trip. I'll tell you everything a little later on. My marriage fell apart and I decided then and there I was moving to Atlanta."

"So did mine. And you know what? I'm glad to get out of it."

We talked for another thirty minutes and then I said, "You are not going to believe this." That was our traditional greeting for each other, and I continued, "I woke up this morning packing my bags to move to Atlanta. So, I'm on my way, make room for me 'cause I'll be there tonight."

She laughed out the words, "You don't even have to explain. I knew something was going on with you and somehow I knew you'd be coming so   I got an extra bedroom just in case. We're going to be roomies again, girl! If you leave now you should be here in twelve hours, I'll see you tonight."

She gave me the address and I was on my way to a new life in Atlanta. The best part of it all was that my best friend was there. We were about to be roommates again, the bad marriages were behind us and we could start anew. I had someone to confide in. I had family waiting!

As I drove to Atlanta, I saw the alpha male wolf running alongside my car.   It was Anaghia.   She was keeping her promise that she would be there for me.   I felt strong and secure and I felt protected and loved.   I knew things would be all right from that day on...and they were.   A few years later, I met and fell in love with my soul mate; his name means Holy Warrior. I started a non-profit corporation that takes people totally out of homelessness and helps senior and disabled citizens live independently.   Anaghia was right! I had a destiny to fulfill. Since meeting and marrying my current husband, I have experienced love on the deepest level possible and I have not had need for my wolf's help but I know the spirit of canis lives.

End! Or, is it?